FAIRIES AND FROSTING - ILLUSTRATED EDITION

BOOK 7 OF THE FAIRY TALES OF THE MAGICORUM

CHRISTINA BAUER

COPYRIGHT

Newton, MA 02464
www.monsterhousebooks.com
ISBN 9781945723346

DEDICATION

For All Those Who Kick Ass, Take Names, and Read Books

CONTENTS

BONUS ILLUSTRATIONS

ALSO BY CHRISTINA BAUER

APPENDIX

6. The Brutal Time

7. Armageddon

8. Quasi Redux

9. Clockwork Igni

10. Lady Reaper

11. Angry Gods

12. Phantom Corsair

Angelbound Lincoln

The Angelbound experience as told by Prince Lincoln

1. Duty Bound

2. Lincoln

3. Trickster

4. Baculum

5. Angelfire

6. Rixa

7. Mordred

Angelbound Offspring

The next generation takes on Heaven, Hell, and everything in between

1. Maxon

2. Portia

3. Zinnia

4. Rhodes

5. Kaps

6. Mack

7. Huntress

** This is a completed series.*

Angelbound Xavier

Xavier's story

1. Archenemy

2. Archnemesis

3. Archangel

Pixieland Diaries

Sassy pixie Calla loves elf prince Dare. Too bad he hasn't noticed her. Yet.

1. Pixieland Diaries
2. Calla
3. Dare
4. Winter Prince
5. Ley Queen

Dimension Drift

Dystopian adventures with science, snark, and hot aliens

1. Scythe
2. Umbra
3. Alien Minds
4. ECHO Academy

This is a completed series.

Beholder

Where a medieval farm girl discovers necromancy and true love

1. Cursed
2. Concealed
3. Cherished
4. Crowned
5. Cradled

This is a completed series.

FAIRIES AND FROSTING

ELLE

I stand before Manhattan's Apex Towers. Imagine a Sharpie pen and a spaceship making a skyscraper baby. That's the Apex. My boyfriend, Alec, waits nearby.

"This place is huge," he declares. "Hard to believe it's empty."

"Only the top levels are occupied," I state. "My inside source confirmed everything. Right after Lady R bought the towers, she sealed off most floors."

Lady R (aka the Lady) is the world's most powerful internet influencer. And when a billion folks follow your webcasts, it seems you can do kooky stuff with real estate and it's no problem. We're here today so the Lady can interview Alec about his company, Le Charme Jewelers, and its upcoming Glass Slipper Festival. In less than a week, the festival will launch Le Charme's new product line… and hopefully, keep the company from going bankrupt.

No pressure.

I give Alec the side-eye. "Speaking of the Lady, do you think she'll actually interview you this time?"

"I'd say the chances are fifty-fifty. You?"

"By my calculations, it's ninety-eight percent likely that she bags on us both."

The Lady requested my presence today because—as her email put it—*Alec is Manhattan's most eligible bachelor and everyone wants to meet his new woman.* That's code for, *I'll plug the stupid Glass Slipper Festival if I can ask Elle embarrassing questions.* Which is fine with me. Hell, I even shaved my legs for the occasion.

But now that the interview approacheth, a thread of worry winds its way through me, along with an ugly question.

Am I really ready for a billion views?

I inspect myself in the building's glass exterior.

Blonde tresses? *Check.*

Blue eyes? *Check again.*

Nervous energy? *Check, check, and check.*

For his part, Alec sports tawny hair, an easy smile, and a jeans-n-sport coat combo. Both of us are eighteen in calendar years and a thousand when it comes to life experiences. Case in point: Alec just escaped a magical prison hidden inside a gemstone. I'm not even kidding.

I shift my weight from foot to foot. That dainty thread of worry is quickly becoming a transcontinental cable of anxiety. Why did I wear this outfit again? I'm not Sundress Girl. My style is more, *let's steal things while wearing wacky disguises.* I fluff my hair and turn to Alec. "How do I look?"

Alec scans me carefully from head to toe. "Like a princess."

That's a good answer.

Going on tiptoe, I brush a kiss across his full mouth.

Alec smacks his lips. "That was the best part of my morning." Glancing down, he checks his watch. "Sadly, the not-so-pleasant bit is coming up. Our interview with Lady R starts soon."

"If she cancels on us again—"

"Hey, she might not." Alec flashes me his best surfer-boy grin. It's almost enough to derail my question, but not quite.

"Yet if she does, what new B-S excuse do you think she'll shovel our way?"

"Oooh, good question." Alec rocks on his heels. "So far, she's nixed us because of a bad hair day, rabid mouse in her bathroom, and a sudden case of pink eye."

"You have to give her points for creativity in lying."

And I would know. Most of my days are spent conning people with elaborate heists in order to *un*-steal jewels. Long story.

Alec purses his lips. "I'm going with *excessive cramping.*"

"Good call. I'll say *alien abduction.*"

"Ding, ding, ding! We have a winner." Alec's phone beeps. Now that he's CEO, it does that a lot. He checks the screen and winces.

"Bad news?"

"The festival takes place in less than a week and—" Alec flips the screen to face me "—fifty-six percent of registrants canceled last night."

I scan the screen. Sure enough, that's what it says. *Eep.*

Alec shakes his head. "Why is this happening now?"

"You know how stuff blows up on social media. Word's going around that the festival will suck."

Which it won't. We'll have music, fashion, and free cupcakes with cream cheese frosting. That last part is my idea. You can't cheap out on sweets.

Alec resets his phone into his pocket and checks the top level of the Apex. "We need extra buzz for the festival. The Lady simply *must* come through today."

I roll my eyes. "Meh."

Alec shoots me a look of mock-surprise. "Meh?"

"Meh."

Alec's mouth winds into a sneaky grin. "How can you *meh* me at a time like this?"

"Because even if the Lady cancels, we'll *still* get the interview. It just won't happen with her *active* participation."

In other words, Alec and I have a contingency plan. Which is actually more of a group caper. My specialty.

"You're rather confident." That's what Alec says, but the gleam in his eyes adds that he wants to get me naked.

And I very much like that look.

I step closer, pausing when our mouths are only a breath apart. "I know we can do this."

In truth, I'm not sure that we can accomplish anything today. Still, I never express doubts this early in a caper. It's just bad form.

Alec bobs his brows. "In that case, the sooner we enter the building, the faster we'll know what happens next." He offers me his arm. "Shall we?"

I wrap my hand around Alec's elbow. "Let's."

As we step toward the entrance, I come to a sweet realization. Namely, I've pulled off hundreds of heists over the years. But if the Lady blows us off again this morning?

Behold the masterwork.

APEX TOWERS

2

ELLE

*A*lec and I sashay into Apex. The place reminds me of a science fiction movie where a space cruiser is set up for thousands of people… only there's no one around.

The lobby is all empty benches, dry fountains, and echoing spaces. The walls are marred by the scraped-off signs from lost businesses. Every doorway and exit is boarded up, except for the fancy bronze elevator that reads *penthouse level.*

A lone guard sits behind a twisty steel desk that pointedly blocks access to the elevator doors. He's a gangly fellow with Art Garfunkel hair, an overly large forehead, teeny brown eyes, and tons of freckles. He looks up as we approach.

"Halt!" cries the guard.

Alec and I stop in place. I give the guy a friendly wave. "Morning, Rueben."

As fate would have it, Rueben's red hair is the color of a perfectly roasted corned beef sandwich. It's enough to make me hungry.

Rueben narrows his eyes. "How do you know my name?"

"It's written on your shirt," states Alec.

Rueben checks his ID tag. "Oh, I always forget about that." He leans back in his chair. "You two have magical auras... I can sense it."

"Yes," confirms Alec. "We've had this conversation already. You met us both no less than three time—"

Rueben holds up his super-long hand. "Now, don't interrupt me. Let me guess."

I fight the urge to groan. Rueben is one of the many annoying things about visiting the Apex. The only tenant here is the Lady. As a result, this guard has lots of alone-time on his hands. He tends to drag stuff out.

Rueben taps his pointy chin. "You two are members of the Magicorum. That means you're either shifters, wizards, or fae. So which is it?" He pauses dramatically before pointing toward Alec. "Ah, ha! You're a gemstone wizard who casts spells with diamonds, rubies, and the like. Am I right?"

"You're correct," replies Alec.

Next, Rueben turns to me. "And what would you be?"

"Not a troll," I answer. *Only because that's what Rueben always guesses.*

"I have it!" Rueben claps. "You're a troll!"

"I am fae, but I'm not a troll."

Rueben narrows his eyes. "Are you sure?"

"Trolls are what we call shadowcoe. They're both nocturnal and not very human-looking." I gesture across myself. "I may stay up late, but I've got the human thing down."

Rueben sniffs. "Bah. You could be using a glamour spell to hide your true appearance." He drums his fingers on the desktop.

With that, one thing is official: *This is taking way too long.* Waiting around isn't helping my already-overburdened nervous system. So I decide to cut Rueben off before he gets to his next favorite subject.

"In case you're wondering," I begin. "Alec and I are both part of the Magicorum, so we're also drawn onto a fairy tale life template. Mine is Cinderella. Alec is Prince Charming."

Rueben frowns. "There you go, ruining all my fun. I wanted to guess your templates next."

"You don't say," I deadpan.

"I can still take a stab at your names." Rueben snaps his fingers at Alec. "Ah, I've got it. You're Alec Le Charme."

"That's right." Alec nods. "As I tried to explain before, we've met previously. Three times."

Rueben ignores Alec and turns to me. "And you're Bimbo."

I roll my eyes. "No, my name's Elle."

Rueben scrunches up his face. "But I thought…"

"*Bimbo* is what Lady R calls me. My real name is Elle. And we've covered this before, too."

"Ah." Rueben nods slowly. "I'll make a note so I don't forget that again." I can't help but notice how the guard doesn't write down a thing.

"Moving on," says Alec smoothly. "Elle and I have an interview in the penthouse with Lady R." He gestures toward the datapad on the guard's desktop. "Please activate the elevator."

"I need to check the Lady's schedule first." Rueben flips through a few screens. "Ah, here it is."

"Excellent," says Alec. "I knew the Lady would come through for us." He steps toward the elevator doors.

Rueben holds up his hand, palm forward. "Not so fast. The Lady must cancel all her appointments today. Dead goldfish. Bathroom funeral. It's a big deal."

I can't believe this.

Or rather, I totally can.

"Come again?" asks Alec. "Did you say, cancel?"

"Yes," confirms Rueben. "Didn't Grayson tell you?" The way he says the name Grayson, it's how I might say the words, *voluntary enema.*

Here's the situation on Grayson. As a member of the Magicorum, the Lady is an elf with a Rapunzel life template. Grayson is her Tower Tithe—meaning the poor shlub who caters to the

Lady's every whim. Mostly, the Lady does whatever she wants, never tells a soul, and then uses Grayson as an all-purpose scapegoat. I know all this for one simple reason: for weeks, Grayson's been my inside contact at the Apex.

"I knew it!" Rueben stares pointedly at me. "Grayson didn't tell you anything, did she?"

"It's like this," I reply. "If you suspect that Grayson failed to inform us, then that's *not* what you *shouldn't* believe."

"Ah." Rueben frowns. "I guess that's… oh."

One great thing about being fae: I know how to derail trains of thought. In this case, Rueben couldn't look more stunned if I hit him in the face with a baseball bat.

Alec sets his hand in his right pocket. It's one of his best *menswear magazine-style* poses. "Do you mind calling Lady to double-check if her fish funeral is over? This interview is very important to me."

In reply, Rueben slowly drags the morning paper across his desktop and scans the headline. "Oh, my! I'm just noticing this now."

Sure, he is.

The guard flips around the paper so Alec and I can read it easily. "Is this why the interview with Lady R is so crucial?"

There's no missing the big headline.

Le Charme Jewelers Almost Bankrupt

And beneath that sits a smaller article that's also not-too-pleasant.

The Glass Slipper Festival is Le Charme's last chance to drive sales…
but will anyone attend?

"You don't need to answer," adds Rueben. "Your festival is almost here. The Lady could really help you."

"Yuppers," I confirm.

Leaning forward, I set my palms on the guard's table. It's a power pose that I use in situations such as this one.

"Listen, babe," I begin. "The Lady needs to keep her word and do this morning's interview. It's bad luck to screw people over. She might get struck by lightning." *Or a caper.*

Rueben chuckles. "Just keep coming back. She'll let you in eventually. Maybe. Some folks have returned fifty times already."

"Wow," I state. "Is that ever rude."

"When you have a billion followers, you can do whatever you want." Rueben flips over a glossy magazine and taps another article. "Seen this?"

Again, there's no missing the brightly-colored text.

Lady R is a market maker! She calls the Bling Me 'the hottest jeweler around'... and the company sells two million necklaces in twenty-four hours

"Yes, I've read that story," confirms Alec. Somehow, he's still working his sunny surfer-guy vibe.

"Want to know something else?" asks Rueben.

This time I reply. "Nope."

Rueben keeps going anyway. "The Lady interviewed Bling Me the very *first time* they came here." The guard focuses on Alec. "You should play the game."

Ah, the game.

In other words, the Lady loves bribes of the magical variety. She's an elf, but not a very powerful one when it comes to casting spells. The Lady always asks for relics and potions that help with mind control… and boost her viewership. But Alec's been on the receiving end of that kind of magic. Needless to say, he won't play *the game.*

Sure enough, Alec shakes his head. "We've covered this before. If the Lady wants payment for her time, that's fine. The Bling Me boys are regular humans. They pay in cash. But I won't hand over certain kinds of magic."

"What?" Rueben's eyes widen. "I didn't say the Lady was enchanting people to watch her videos."

"And we didn't accuse her of that," I add.

Although we all know that's happened. And it's totally illegal. After all, if Alec could use magic to fix Le Charme's problems, he'd have done it ages ago. But the MITRE agency polices the Magicorum. If you use spells to manipulate humans for profit, then you can end up in a supernatural jail.

"I don't want any trouble." Rueben points to the door. "You two need to leave."

"Of course," says Alec. Turning in unison, he and I march toward the door.

But in truth? We aren't going anywhere. This is the very outcome I'd been hoping for. Our crew and heist are ready to go.

Operation Web Beastie is about to begin.

3

ALEC

Elle and I step onto the sidewalk. While we've been inside the Apex, the morning has kicked into high gear. Cloud cover has burned away. Sidewalks and streets are filled with more traffic.

Craning my neck, I scan the top level of the Apex Towers once more. *The Lady's up there.* Sure, I'd hoped she'd keep her word. That said, I can't pretend to be shocked that she backed out.

At least, Elle can launch her plan now... and my woman is never more beautiful than when she's working a caper. Before we dated, I spent hours watching security footage of Elle robbing my office. *Love at first heist.*

"You know what this means," I announce.

Elle rubs her palms together in the universal hand movement of evil geniuses everywhere. "Time for Operation Web Beastie."

Of course, I know her plan by heart. That said, I adore watching Elle describe it. There's a special kind of gleam that shines in her eyes while scheming. It's hypnotic.

"Give me the plan one more time," I request.

"There are four steps," replies Elle. "One. Distract the guard. Two. Take the elevator to the Lady's penthouse. Three. Get past the apartment sentry and reach the Lady's inner sanctum. And four. Convince the Lady to talk up the Glass Slipper Ball on her webcast."

"Perfect." I pull her to me. My senses become overwhelmed with the delicious sensation of Elle's body pressing against mine. I slowly run my palm up her bare back.

"Did I mention how I like this sundress?" I ask. "Because I really do."

Elle smirks. "Keep touching me that way, and I might just skip Operation Web Beastie and drag you back to my place."

"It's tempting," I state. "But I can't allow such lovely plans to go to waste." I run my nose along the length of hers. "Let's check in on our first step."

Moving back, I pull out my cell and type a message to one of our accomplices.

MagicMan: Hey
ElfBoy: Ho

ElfBoy is none other than Prince Jacoby, one of Elle's long-time friends who's now part of our crew for this mission. Jacoby's an elf who specializes in Fortitude magic, which is the ability to leverage the power of large—and often magical—animals. I quickly type my reply.

MagicMan: lady bagged on us
ElfBoy: shocker?

Jacoby then sends a gif of a cat coughing up a hairball. The flashing text reads, *Not*.

I chuckle. While we were planning this mission, Jacoby was

convinced the Lady would bag on us. I'm sure he had this cat retort ready to go.

MagicMan: r u and Agatha ready?

Agatha is Elle's stepsister. Contrary to the fairy tale, Agatha is actually really cool. She met Jacoby and now they're dating.

ElfBoy: yup just need the words
MagicMan: 1 sec...

By referring to *the words*, Jacoby is asking me to type the special passphrase that will officially launch our scheme.

Jacoby and Agatha are in charge of distracting the guard and activating the elevator. That said, these two have been very hush-hush about some specifics in their part of the scheme. It'll be fun to see what they come up with.

I refocus on Elle. "Jacoby's ready to go. Any reason not to give him the passphrase?"

Elle opens her mouth to reply. Yet before she can speak, lightning flashes across the sky, followed by a low roll of thunder.

I frown. This surprise storm is unexpected. Still, Manhattan is its own microclimate. Strange things take place here all the time. Pretty routine stuff.

My inner magic disagrees. It senses a new power in the air. All the gemstones in my pockets change. Before they were light as feathers. Now the rocks seem to weigh a ton. Fresh energy skitters across my skin. Closing my eyes, I tap into my inner power while grasping a few gemstones. Those enchanted rocks cry out in my mind.

Beware the magic.

"Elle, do you sense anything strange?"

No reply.

Opening my eyes, I find Elle standing perfectly still. Her eyes are glassy and unfocused. Worry pounds through my nervous system.

What's wrong with Elle?

ELLE

*A*ll the lightning and thunder are downright odd. A heavy sense of foreboding fills the air.

This is no freak storm.

One by one, the people around me vanish from view. Pedestrians fade from the sidewalk. Cars sit empty on the street. The world becomes deserted, except for me.

Uh oh.

My mind churns through every type of spell that could be behind all this. I rule out an illusion enchantment; my mind feels perfectly clear. Then I notice a manhole cover pop up a few inches in the middle of the street. The yellow eyes of a troll blink at me before the cover closes. Which leads to one conclusion.

Not everyone is disappearing.

That narrows things down.

I recall another time when most people seemed to vanish while leaving certain kinds of supernaturals behind. It happened back when I was in Egypt and releasing warden magic.

Could warden magic be at work again here?

Like rain on the desert, magic has its own way of replenishing itself on Earth. Only instead of a downpour, magic uses folks like me. I was born with fae warden energy which I eventually set loose at the pyramids of Egypt. And I wasn't the only one, either. Alec did the same for warlocks. His friend, Knox, released the power of shifters. And my bestie, Bry, discharged some of all three types.

But I'm the only one with any warden energy left. Call it a side effect of my magic coming from the fae. We never do what's expected.

With every passing second, my remaining warden magic goes more nutso inside me. It's definitely reacting to the power all around. Within seconds, my body feels so jittery, it's as if I were sticking a fork in an electrical socket (and yes, I had to do that once on a heist. Not cool.)

No question about it. *This is active warden energy. But what's it doing?*

Suddenly, the ground rumbles beneath my feet. Great obelisks break through the pavement, their towering shapes filling the landscape. Each one is clear as glass.

Then they all change.

The obelisks transform into hefty trees with brown trunks and branches that are heavily laden with emerald leaves. The streets and buildings of New York melt into green grass and dark soil. One second, I stand in Manhattan. The next moment, I'm surrounded by a forest.

It takes me a full minute to adjust to my new environment. Crows caw as they fly through low branches. The overcast sky sends shadows all around. Every so often, multi-colored bolts of lightning burst inside the dark cloud cover. I try to cast spell after spell, hoping to figure out what's going on.

Nothing works. I can't even get so much as a single sparkle of fairy dust to show up.

So annoying.

Then I catch the sound of rustling nearby. A fresh wave of shock zings through my nervous system.

I'm not alone.

MAGIC FOREST

5

ELLE

I step around in a slow circle. "Hello?"

Long seconds pass before a man's voice reverberates through the shadows.

"Greetings, Elle."

Eek.

Sometimes, all my years of experience with the seedy side of life just pay off. Because in this case? A mystery dude only said two words—*Greetings, Elle*—and yet, it's still enough for me to know the guy is totally evil.

Fortunately, I have rules for such situations. The first is to get the bad guys talking. If this mystery man were going to attack, he would have done it already. Instead, I'm guessing this evildoer wants to blab.

Happy to oblige.

It's tempting to ask, *what's up with this magic forest?* But that would be a rookie mistake. In situations like this one, it's best to start off with easy questions and work your way up.

I cup my hand by my mouth. "How do you know my name?"

"Everyone knows Elle Cynder. You're the girl who poisons

everything. You're not really a Cinderella. Not even a genie. No true power moves through you, whether fae, witch, or warden."

I set my first on my hip. "I have extra powers because I'm super fabulous."

Which is a bit of a lie. Some days, I'd like to fit in a neat box that's marked Cinderella. Or Genie. Or anything. But that's not me. In general, that fact doesn't bother me. Until some asshat brings it up. *Like this guy.*

I force in a few calming breaths. *Focus, Elle.* The fact that this mystery man knows my name means he's done some research. Which is no big deal. The guy could open a web browser and discover the name of Alec Le Charme's new girlfriend.

That said, getting my magical profile is a bit trickier. That's not exactly common knowledge. I have my rogue warden energy. But that's not all. From my mother, I inherited fairy summoning magic which I use to get help from small animals. My father gave me enchanter powers that I can tap into and connect with other witches and wizards.

However, thanks to Grayson, I happen to know that the Lady has all this info, too. So it's tough to find out my magical history, but not impossible.

Which brings up an idea.

The more I think about it, the more I'm convinced the Lady is somehow teamed up with this mystery guy. After all, I get dragged to his magical forest right outside the Apex. Coincidence? I think not.

"What do you want from me?" I ask.

"To watch you fail yet another time."

"So you're what… my supernatural stalker?"

"Not by choice."

It's tempting to say, *that's because the Lady is making you do this, sucker.* But that would give away that I'm on to him. And there's no benefit to me revealing that yet. So I keep my reply non-committal.

I mock frown. "Poor you."

"I should say so," adds the man. "Being close to you is a dangerous place to be. No one stays near you for long, do they? Your mother died of cancer. Dear Daddy expired from a broken heart."

Before, I thought it was intrusive for this guy to know my magical profile. But this level of information is way more than personal… it's cruel.

"Alec is next, don't you think?" adds the man. "And once he's gone, what about your precious friends? As the saying goes, off with their heads!"

My analytical side wants to focus on that last phrase: *Off with their heads!* That's a saying associated with the Queen of Hearts. The fact that the man is using it now feels important.

But my thinking side doesn't stand a chance at this point. My emotions are too riled up. Mostly because I do feel like I'm poison to anyone around me. And I often wonder if Alec would be safer with someone else in his life. It's the same with my friends.

My temper quickly hits a boiling point. I want to strike back. And the only weapon I can think of is my knowledge of what's really happening here.

"You think you're so clever," I declare. "I've already figured out who's really pulling your strings. The Lady. Well, you can tell your mistress that it takes a lot more than some nasty talk to bother me."

In reply, I'm hoping for a snide remark. Maybe even a curse or two thrown in my direction. But the mystery guy starts laughing instead.

"The Lady?" he asks. "And who might that be?"

"A Rapunzel life template who lives in the Apex towers? Does that ring any bells?"

"No. And if I did know some Rapunzel, so you seriously

believe she could control me? If so, you're even dumber than I thought."

My heart sinks. You never know for sure with bad guys, but my instincts tell me that this guy really doesn't know the Lady. How could I have misjudged this situation so badly? If this isn't a magical scheme with the Lady, then what's at work?

Lightning bolts strike the ground nearby, startling me. Peals of thunder boom with such force, it sets my ears ringing. Around me, the trees turn back into glassy obelisks before sinking into the ground again.

One final flash of lightning strikes. This time, the bolt is so bright that white splotches blot out my vision. When I can see again, I find myself back on the Manhattan sidewalk. Alec stands beside me. His eyes are wide with worry.

"Are you all right?"

"Yes," I reply. "What happened to me?"

"I found you staring off into space. You didn't hear me when I called for you. I've seen spells like this at work before. You were catatonic."

"How long was I like that?"

"Less than a minute." He pulls me into a hug. "Still, it scared me half to death."

I lean into his embrace. Alec is a good hugger. "I got pulled to a magical forest. Some creepy guy said he knew me and was watching me."

"Any idea who it was?"

"At first, I thought the Lady set everything up. But later, I decided that theory is crap. Honestly? I have no idea who this guy might be."

Alec's features turn unreadable. "Do you want to call off this morning's caper?"

And he means it. With so much on the line, Alec really would cancel everything for me.

"Never." I lift my chin. "Let's do this."

Alec checks his phone again. "Jacoby's still ready. Should I give him the passphrase?"

"Type away."

Alec's thumbs speed over his cell phone as he both recites the phrase out loud and gives it to Jacoby. "Begin the badassery." A moment passes before Alec meets my gaze once more. "It is begun."

At first, nothing happens. Then Jacoby's familiar voice echoes down the sidewalk.

"Kashvi! Kashvi! Come here!"

Turning, I follow the source of my friend's voice… and gasp at what I find. Sure, I suspected that Jacoby would involve some kind of large animal in his diversion.

But I wasn't prepared for this. Suddenly, all I can see is Kashvi.

KASHVI

6

ALEC

New Yorkers barely notice the unusual. Yet the locals do stare as a colorful baby elephant marches down the sidewalk. Soon a small crowd follows the pachyderm. No one even notices Jacoby in his black pants and matching shirt. Which is saying something. As an elf, Jacoby exudes the kind of tall, dark, and handsome mojo that humans find fascinating.

Kashvi parks right before the Apex front door, blocking all entry. The human parade stops as well. Some folks snap selfies. Others chatter excitedly.

Time for the next phase of the plan… And this bit uses magic.

Jacoby raises his hands to waist level. A sphere of power appears between his palms. Humans can't see this orb, but it contains magic that will hide Kashvi from all humans except Rueben.

The sphere bursts and the spell is cast. The humans around Kashvi meander away. Even better, they all clear out their phone pics as they go. Which makes this one of Jacoby's best creations. His casting not only hides Kashvi, but it also erases any digital trace she was ever here.

As for me and Elle, we speed to our preset reconnaissance

spot. The Apex offers plenty of hiding places in its twisty metal outer frame. Elle and I conceal ourselves in a place where Rueben can't see us, yet we can watch both the guard and Kashvi.

She really is a cute elephant.

Seconds later, Rueben rises, crosses the lobby, and shoves the door open. It isn't easy, but the guard is eventually able to squeeze outside.

"What are you doing here?" asks Rueben.

"Isn't it obvious?" Jacoby gestures toward the elephant. "I'm giving Kashvi a walk."

"That isn't a dog."

Jacoby shoots the guard a sideways glance. "Why would you think it's a dog? Are you quite all right, sir?"

"I'm fine," says Rueben. "You're the one who's walking an elephant!"

"Excellent." Jacoby beams. "So you accept this isn't a canine. Progress! Allow me to explain some basic facts about pachyderms. To begin with, elephants have more than 150,000 muscles in their trunks…"

"Ah, Jacoby." Elle sighs as her friend continues his tirade. "I've been on the receiving end of Jacoby's *teacher mode*. He can do this for hours."

I nod. "The plan is moving along well."

With this realization, a fresh round of excitement charges through my limbs. I'm not a singing man, but I have the odd temptation to belt out *We Are The Champions*.

Next up: Agatha.

Elle's stepsister slips out from her own metal hiding place. She has red hair, green eyes, and the kind of grace that only elves can manage.

With fast motions, Agatha pulls up a new sphere of power and tosses it toward the building's exterior. A door-sized hole instantly opens in the lobby's glass wall. A moment later, Agatha is inside the building and casting another spell. This time, the shimmer of light means she's changing her appearance. Agatha becomes the perfect replica of Rueben.

Yes!

With the guard occupied and Agatha in place, it's time for Elle and I to enter the Apex. We use the same process as Agatha. Within seconds, Elle and I stroll up to the guard's desk. Sure enough, Agatha looks just like Rueben, except for the eyes, which she's kept a vibrant shade of green.

"Your appointment is confirmed," says Agatha-Rueben. "Allow me to open the elevator." Agatha taps a few codes into her data-pad. The metal doors slide open with a soft chime. "Enjoy your interview."

Elle beams. "You're amazing."

I wink. "The green eyes are a nice touch, too."

Agatha blushes. "Thank you."

Elle and I enter the elevator. The moment we're inside, my phone buzzes. Sadly, there's no need to check the screen. It's surely another message from the Board of Directors, begging me to sign the bankruptcy paperwork for Le Charme Jewelers.

Images appear in my mind. I picture the thousands of employees and their families. Some have served Le Charme for more than forty years. And then, there are the seven dwarves who dig up our gemstones. They've been Le Charme's miners for centuries. Closing Le Charme would take away their purpose in life. For dwarves, that's a magical death sentence.

This interview with the Lady simply has to work.

I shut off my phone and focus on the task ahead. After all, Rueben was right about one thing—Bling Me started off as two guys in a basement. But thanks to the Lady, they're now a multi-million dollar company. If I can just get the Lady to keep her word, then Le Charme might take off as well.

7

ELLE

*D*ing! In my mind, I know the elevator stops with a cute little chime. But at this moment, it feels more like the booming of a cannon. Mostly because it signifies that we're now in phase two of my master plan.

Get past the interior sentry.

In other words, Alec and I need to sneak by Grayson. Since she's my accomplice, you'd think this would be easy.

Not so.

The elevator doors quietly slide open to reveal our problem. The reception room is a large space whose walls appear to be covered in half-spheres. It could be a *funky style* thing, but it isn't. Behind every half-orb, there sits a 180-degree camera. All video feeds go to the Lady. And she controls the exits as well.

The only way we're getting past Grayson is with another diversion that's so overwhelming, the Lady won't notice as we leave.

Once Alec and I step out of the elevator, the reception

chamber goes dark. A spotlight beams down from the ceiling, surrounding Alec in a halo of light. A voice echoes through the darkness.

"Welcome, Alec Le Charme. You have been granted an audience with the great Lady R."

Another pillar of light cascades onto me as well. "Hello, Elle Cynder."

The lights flicker on to reveal a large and empty space. Sure enough, there's no furniture here—only walls that are covered in half-spheres. Now I know what it's like to be surrounded in bubble wrap.

An elf stands in the center of the room. She wears a formal gown from Faerie Lands and holds both a pink pearl and a white scepter. Her face is pleasant and soothing, but not startlingly beautiful like many elves. And her expression is completely unreadable.

It's Grayson.

I have to hand it to this girl. No one would suspect she's been my inside contract for this whole caper.

"Welcome," she says. A dark look sparks in her green eyes as she adds five words.

"I shall now explain everything."

GRAYSON

ELLE

Many royal elves have their servants recite a little speech before allowing visitors into their homes. It's a way of saying, *hey, look at my fancypants.*

Sure enough, Grayson launches into one of these tirades with the same level of excitement I wielded while shaving my legs this morning.

Which is to say, *none.*

"I am Grayson Eyre, a Tower Tithe. This item—" here she raises the pink pearl in her right hand "—symbolizes my eternal servitude to the great Lady R. You may now ooh and ahh at how lucky I am."

Alec and I share a dry look. *She can't be serious.*

A crackle sounds as hidden speakers come to life. A shrill voice echoes through the large room. "Heed the ugly wench! Do what she says!"

That would be the Lady.

At the mention of the word *ugly*, Grayson visibly shivers. *Looks like the Lady hit a nerve.* In my opinion, Grayson has a gentle beauty that doesn't call attention to itself at first. She's more the quiet kind of gorgeous that grows on you over time.

The Lady's voice sounds once more from hidden speakers. "Did you hear what I said? I want some noises, people!"

Since our distraction hasn't arrived yet, it's not like we have much choice here.

"Oooh," I say.

"Ahhh," adds Alec.

"Thank you," says Grayson. "In my left hand, I hold the wand of eternal smiting. It is used to punish those who enter here without permission."

Which is a total lie. Grayson told me she got that wand at Target. It's as magical as my shoe.

A long pause follows. I felt pretty sure this would be a place that the Lady would want to screech, but it seems like I'm wrong. Alec and I share a long look followed by a short shrug.

"We have permission," says Alec.

"It's not like we invited ourselves," I add.

The Lady's voice echoes through the chamber at a higher volume than ever before. "No, you don't have permission! My favorite goldfinch is dead!"

I raise my hand. "I thought it was your goldfish."

"That's what I said! Now I must perform the necessary rites for little Fishy Poo and YOU MUST GO."

But Alec and I don't leave. It seems like our diversion is running a little late. We must stall for time.

"I can see them on the cameras," yells the Lady. "They aren't leaving."

"Someone needs to activate the elevator," says Alec.

Which is some good thinking. When it comes to making up stalling tactics on the fly, Alec is a natural.

"Just push the button," calls the Lady.

"Button?" I make a great show of scanning the walls around the elevator. There is, in fact, a very large button on the right-hand side. I ignore the hell out of it. "I don't see anything."

Alec makes a big show of looking as well. "Dang! I can't find it, either. Are you sure there's a button around here?"

"Grayson!" The Lady's voice is extra-screechy now. "Push the button for these fools."

I'm starting to worry that we're running out of plausible stalling tactics when it happens.

Ding!

The elevator chimes once again. This time, the doors open to reveal none other than Bry and Knox. Both wear blue overalls with the name Mouse In The House Exterminators embroidered on the bib.

Bry steps off first. She's a werewolf, Sleeping Beauty life template, and my good friend. She looks like her fairy tale name-sake as well, what with her long brown hair, intelligent blue eyes, and royal demeanor. For the purposes of this caper, she's playing the role of Exterminator One.

Right behind Bry comes Knox. Even though he's wearing the equivalent of an adult onesie, Knox still oozes bad boy swagger. That totally works, considering how Knox is an alpha werewolf. I have him playing the role of Exterminator Two.

"We're here about the mice," says Knox.

"WHAT?" The Lady's voice takes on a note of hysteria.

I push down on the urge to rub my hands together and say, *mwhah hah hah*. Grayson totally hooked me up with the right intel. The Lady hates mice.

"There are no mice in the Apex!" If the Lady keeps screaming like this, I worry she'll snap a vocal cord.

Closing my eyes, I call upon my Cinderella summoning magic. We're supposed to use it to inspire small animals into doing housework, only I've adapted it over the years.

Once I feel my fairy power rising within me, I reach out to my little buddies.

You're up.

Turns out, the Lady is right. There are no mice in the Apex. Until now.

Sure enough, my favorite mouse Gustav squeezes his way out from under a floorboard.

"Hello!" He cries, then remembers his role. "I mean, squeak!"

If I thought the Lady was losing it before, now she really goes berserk. "ARGH!"

"Should I leave?" asks Grayson quietly.

"No, you little idiot," cries the Lady. "Stay with the exterminators. Get rid of the mice!"

Gustav sets his pinkies in either side of his mouth and lets out a high-pitched whistle. Hundreds of mice bound out from behind the walls to cover the floor in one seething mass of fur. Bry and Knox make motions to catch them but are always too slow.

The Lady's reaction is both predictable and lovely. "AAAAAAAAAAAAAARGH!"

Alec leans in to whisper in my ear. "This is our cue."

"Got it."

While all the mayhem continues, Alec and I magically unlock the exit and slip through a maze of hallways. Soon we reach the room where the Lady awaits. The chamber itself is made of magical boxes, each one stacked on the other. The surface of every square shows a slightly different view of the reception chamber. As we enter, the screens all go dark.

The moment that happens, the Lady stops screaming. Little by little, she turns to face us. Seeing her up close, I can report that the Lady is the classic kind of elf.

Refined features.

Pointy ears.

Flashy dress.

Big mouth.

A full minute passes before the Lady speaks again.

"Mice," she says slowly. "And you're a Cinderella life template. I should have guessed."

I can't help but grin. *Here comes the fun.*

LADY R

9

ALEC

I have to hand it to her. The Lady's doing a good job of pretending that the horde of mice in her reception room doesn't bother her anymore. But there's a telltale twitch by her mouth that reveals her true emotions.

"Grayson should never have allowed you in here," declares the Lady.

Elle warned me about the Everybody Hates Grayson program that the Lady is running. I won't play along.

"You ordered Grayson to deal with your mouse problem," I counter. "We all heard it over the loudspeaker. And Grayson's doing what you asked of her right now."

"I can call Grayson in here, if you like," offers Elle.

"No!" The Lady takes in a long breath. "I mean, that's not necessary. Grayson is fine where she is. You two are not. I wish you to leave my presence at once. I'm not interviewing anyone today."

Elle and I don't move an inch toward the door. "Let's chat about our options," I begin. "I'm a powerful wizard. Elle's magic is off the charts. Maybe we can come to some kind of agreement, so long as it doesn't involve mind control."

When it comes to the fae, everything is about deals and agreements.

"You two—" here the Lady gestures between us for emphasis "think I'm without magic. But on my show, the popular segment is a little something called Your Favorite Things. Allow me to demonstrate." The Lady cups her hands before her. "Bring me the object Alec most values."

A small orb of crimson light appears on her palms. When the brightness vanishes, the Lady now holding my cell phone.

"How boring," says the Lady. "I was hoping for a gem." She tosses the cell back to me. "Just trust me when I say that you don't want to be on my bad side. Leave now or I will make you pay."

"It's like this," I declare. "We know you've used spells to illegally profit from humans."

The Lady sniffs. "So prove it."

"Well," I say slowly. "You asked me for mind control spells. In emails. And on my cell phone. Many times."

Lady narrows her eyes. I can almost picture the various plans flipping through her mind. "If I'm so terrible, why not report me to MITRE?"

"Because you're not all *that* bad," I reply.

"We did our magical homework," states Elle. "You crave the adoration of humans. Having a bunch of enchanted followers simply won't work. Years ago, you have a plus-one wand of mind control that you used to make people tune in. But that particular magical item ran out of juice long ago. No matter how much you search, you haven't found a replacement wand. These days, your success is all about you."

"That's correct." A small smile rounds the Lady's mouth. "I am rather amazing."

Elle and I have practiced this speech. Now is the part when I go for the close.

"Look," I begin. "I've no desire to turn you over to MITRE.

But you must keep your word about promoting the festival. We came here three times. People's lives are on the line."

The Lady waves her hand dismissively. "Fine. I'll talk up your silly glass slipper thing."

"Great," I declare. "So do it. Now."

10

ELLE

The Lady waves her arm. The wall-boxes slide open. Hover cameras and lights fly out and take their positions.

"We're live in three, two, one!" cries the Lady. Green lights turn on atop all the cameras. The Lady's face brightens with an entrancing grin. "Hello," she says to the invisible crowd. "It's time for Lady R!"

Before, the Lady has been wearing a kind of fitted red swim-cap that's popular with many evil Disney queens. Now she pulls that hat off. Long tresses of blonde hair tumble down her shoulders to snake over the floor. And when I say that's a lot of hair, I mean it's a LOT, a lot.

I can see why the Lady wears a magical cap. That much hair must be a literal pain in the neck.

The Lady saunters over to Alec and asks about the fresh Le Charme line which will be launched at the Glass Slipper Festival. Alec explains how the new designs are all inspired by creations from the magical animates at my parents' old company, Cynder Mercantile.

Which leads to my part of the interview. I'm asked if Alec is a good kisser (answer: great) and how I feel to have landed myself such a wealthy prince (reply: my bank account is actually much better than his). Alec shows off a few pieces from the upcoming line. The Lady grudgingly admits they are lovely.

The livecast ends. Once the cameras and lights go dead, the Lady rounds on us.

"No one makes me keep my word," she snaps. "Watch yourselves."

With that, the Lady saunters out of the room.

"Looks like we made a friend," deadpans Alec.

"Don't worry about that," I counter. "How are registrations?"

Alec pulls out his phone. "Don't you think it's too early to check?" Still, he brings up the screen. "I can't believe it."

"What?"

"We're sold out. The Glass Slipper Festival is now *waiting list only*."

We share a hug and a realization.

What a perfect caper.

All that remains is to gather the whole crew and debrief. For that, we're all supposed to rendezvous at the apartment Alec and Knox share.

It's a little place I like to call the Man Can.

11

ALEC

Elle and I reach the so-called Man Can the old fashioned way... by walking through New York and enjoying the afternoon. In short order, we're back at the apartment.

Sure, we could have used a spell to transport here, but it isn't smart to use magic too often. You can end up unhinged. Take my great Uncle Horace, for instance. He relied on magic for everything. Now Horace lives in a man-sized basket and insists he's a snake. True story.

But I digress.

Now that I'm back in my apartment, I can show Elle one of my greatest decisions, ever. When the werewolf, Hollywood, said he wanted to enter the world of design, I let him take a crack at fixing up the place I share with Knox. As for my roommate, Knox didn't care as long as no one touched his stuff.

For the last few weeks, Hollywood's been working non-stop. All our caper get-togethers have been at Bry and Elle's place.

But now? The time has come for the great reveal.

I set my key in the lock. "Are you ready, Elle?" She knows how Hollywood has been working away.

"So ready."

I push open the door and gesture in my very best game show hostess arm-swoop. "Behold, the new Man Can."

Elle steps inside and freezes. "Umm..."

"What?"

"Is that a twelve-foot-tall picture of me?"

"You don't like it?"

Huh. Maybe hiring a werewolf as my interior designer wasn't the best idea after all.

THE MAN CAN

12

ALEC

*E*lle is playing this rather cool. Personally, I love the massive photo of her on my wall—I can tap her lips every morning as I head to the kitchen. *Talk about good luck.* But Elle's working her poker face right now. It's hard to know if the picture is a hit.

"What do you think?" I ask.

"Wow. That's really big."

This isn't a 'take that thing down now' reaction, but she's not exactly jumping for joy, either.

An idea appears. Perhaps I can guess what she's worried about. Knox and I share this apartment, but the only person pictured here is Elle.

"Look, I checked with Knox already. He didn't want to put up a big picture of Bry."

Elle taps her lips. "Oh."

In other words, the issue here is not the lack of a massive photo of Elle's best friend. That leaves one more option.

"Too much?" I ask.

Not that I'll take it down. If Elle disapproves, I'll magically camouflage it with a forest vista when other people are here. I've gotten used to seeing her first thing in the morning. No way am I giving that up.

Elle tilts her head, turns to me, and smiles. "It's perfect."

The lock jangles as Knox and Bry come in. The pair are out of their industrial onesies. Now Bry wears dress pants and a white shirt. Knox sports jeans, a black T-shirt, and some hefty boots.

Bry pauses as she steps across the threshold. "Oh, my. That's a rather large picture."

"You didn't see this before, either?" asks Elle.

Bry shakes her head.

"Hollywood worked really hard on this," urges Elle.

Bry nods. "Now I understand. It's perfect."

Elle winks. "That's what I said, too."

A warm sense of satisfaction seeps through my rib cage. I knew this redesign would be a hit.

Knocks sound on the door. This time, it's Agatha and Jacoby. There are a lot of hugs and smiles and we celebrate being together again. Even Gustav crawls in from under the floorboards. For her part, Kashvi is back on Jacoby's farm. It seems that baby elephants need their naps.

We order some pizza and rehash our success. The big reveal comes when I share that registration is sold out. Everyone cheers.

For my part, I plunk onto the couch and exhale. After all those weeks of planning, it finally feels as if things are coming together. I won't have to fire loyal employees, and the dwarves can keep the magical work that literally keeps them alive.

Boom!

Thunder blasts through the air, followed by a flash of lightning outside our main window. The air turns heavy with an electric sort of magic.

I rush over to Elle and find her standing stock-still while staring out at nothing in particular.

It's happening again.

ELLE

Flashes of intense light burst across the apartment's interior as more lighting strikes. Now that it's night, the intensity makes my breath catch.

Here we go.

Low rolls of thunder follow. My inner warden magic goes berserk. Electric energy careens through every inch of my body.

The last time this took place, the city street seemed to empty out. Now everyone vanishes from the apartment.

Obelisks rise from the carpet and become trees. The room transforms into a vast forest. The scent of fresh earth surrounds me. Crows swoop through the trees, cawing as they go. Dark clouds hang overhead. Heavy bolts of lightning flash in their depths.

Chills creep up my spine as a realization hits me. *I've seen lightning like that before.* It was back at the pyramids when we all released our warden magic. My mentor and dragon friend, Colonel Mallory the Magnificent, took us to the pyramids in the first place. Ever since then, the colonel's been trying to find out what happened to our warden magic. He believes it disappeared into the ether.

I turn the term over in my mind. *The ether.*

All this time, the colonel assumed the ether was a state, like how water changes from liquid into steam.

But what if the ether is an actual place?

It's more than possible. I scan the clouds more closely. Before, there were occasional bolts churning in the darkness. Now the lightning flares almost constantly.

That means something.

Most likely, it's nothing good.

A figure steps out from the trees. It's an elf with sallow skin and long red robes. Four horns adorn his head. I remember the voice that called to me from the darkness before.

Is this the same man?

"Hello, Elle," he says.

It's the same guy, all right.

I'll never forget that voice. It holds that distinctly sweet tone that barely hides evil intentions.

His mouth winds into a hungry smile. "You've returned to me."

FOUR-HORNED MAN

14

ELLE

I soak in the scene. Here I am, standing in a magical forest with a four-horned man looming before me.

Fortunately, this isn't the weirdest thing that's ever happened to me. By far.

It takes a few moments for my strategic sense to click back into place. Sure, this is a strange-looking guy. But he's still the same mystery dude I met last time. As in, this is someone who shouted threatening stuff to me while hiding behind a bush. Who does that?

This man either wants something… or he's a Lonely Loo like Rueben the guard.

I'm thinking it's the former. *Dude has a plan.* Plus, he's looking at me like I'm a bug and he's the equivalent of a massive boot. If I had to make a bet, I'd say this guy wants revenge.

But for what?

And why am I part of it?

All of which means that my goal hasn't changed from my last visit to this forest. I must get this guy talking. As always, it's best to start with the small stuff.

"You know my name," I begin. "What's yours?"

"You may call me—" here he pauses for dramatic effect "—the bandit." He braces his shoulders, like he's expecting some kind of response to that.

I got nothing.

Still, I store the bandit thing away for later. It's definitely a clue about who this man really is. You know, beyond the fact that he's a drama diva.

"Now that we have names all settled out, let's move on to where we live. I'm a native of New York." I scan the forest. "What's this place?"

"If I didn't tell you last time, what makes you think I'll share that secret now? I'm having far too much fun watching you squirm."

"Two things about that," I counter. "One, I am not squirming. Two, I know this place is the ether. I was just wondering if you'd come clean. But you didn't. Because, for some reason, you've decided you hate me and want to torture me. Now am I right… or am I totally right?"

In reply, the bandit only glares in my direction.

Which means I'm totally right.

The bandit's silence means that I'm winning this little conversation, so I keep right on talking. I gesture toward the sky. "There's still warden magic up there for some reason. It should have settled into either Earth or the Faerie Lands."

Now, I don't expect this guy to blab any real information. Although, I do have about a zillion questions about the ether. Why is it a forest? Is there a house around anywhere? How long has the bandit guy called it home? Time seems to works differently here, so the bandit could have arrived a few minutes ago. He might also have been hanging out for centuries. Tough call.

And all that information would be super interesting to know. Still, it isn't where I really need to focus on here. The larger issue is why the bandit hates my guts. I'm guessing he's trapped in the ether. And considering how I'm one of the folks who sent lightning bolts over his forest home, maybe that's why he's got some Elle issues.

"I can see you have questions," intones the bandit.

"You think?"

"The ether will give you the information you need."

"Vague, but okay."

"Prepare yourself in three, two, one."

Crack!

A massive bolt of lightning strikes the ground nearby. Up close, I'd expect to detect nothing but bright colors.

There's more.

The bolt acts as a window. Within the lightning, I can clearly make out a distinct shape.

The Apex tower.

Both the lightning and vision are only there for a moment. Still, it's enough for me to see the truth.

"The ether is being torn apart," I whisper. "We must have returned too much magic."

"That's right," says the bandit. "These bolts hit every four minutes now. Every strike is a little larger. Each portal stays open a little longer. The many strikes keep the monsters away and move me closer to my goal."

"You want to leave here."

The bandit shrugs. "This realm is filled with horrors. I'm an elf who's aligned to the Unseelie court. I belong in the Faerie Lands with others of my kind. Of course, I wish to leave."

I shake my head. "There's more to it than that."

"Yes, but that's none of your affairs." The bandit steps closer. "Your business is to be the butterfly carcass that wriggles around helplessly while I pull off your wings."

Damn, is that ever nasty.

Now Jacoby is Unseelie fae, same as this guy. But if he were a candy, Jacoby would have a manipulative outer shell around a marshmallow good guy core. But the bandit is the purely evil flavor of Unseelie. He'd dip a rock in chocolate, tell you it's a treat, and then laugh his ass off when you break a tooth. Or worse.

I shiver. Every cell in my body screams that this man is dangerous. I simply must find out what he's up to. A memory appears. In our last conversation, the bandit used a unique phrase.

Off with their heads.

"You serve the Queen of Hearts," I declare.

The bandit practically snarls out his response. "No."

Bingo! Someone doesn't like the queen. Time to press for more information. Perhaps I'll even hit a nerve.

"The queen helped set me up with my boyfriend, Alec. She's a force for good."

The lines of the bandit's face tighten with rage. "The Queen of Hearts is evil incarnate! Once I leave here, I'll destroy her and everything she loves. Including you. Then I'll go after your so-called family as well. You have an elf sister and friend, right? Consider their lives over."

So, that's a nerve, all right.

The bandit stalks closer. "Remember what I said? Sooner or later, you poison anything you touch. Your father. Your mother. Alec. Your friends. Even the Queen of Hearts. It's inevitable."

And sadly, it's also true.

Another crack of lightning strikes nearby. This bolt is the largest one yet. Every detail of the forest becomes searingly clear, from the rivulets of bark that wind down every tree to the yellow eyes that watch from a distance.

Then everything goes dark.

ELLE

The next thing I know, I'm back in the Man Can. Alec stands before me. All our friends wait nearby.

Little by little, Alec gently cradles my face in his palms. His touch is all things warm and grounding. "Are you all right?"

The true answer here would be: *No, I'm all wrong.* The bandit's words still pierce my soul. Alec is a prince. My friends are all pure examples of their magical types and fairy tale templates. I'm broken. Eventually, my defects will damage everyone around me.

Yet I swallow down those facts. Everyone thinks I'm Elle the Unstoppable. And sometimes, I can even join in their fantasy. But if I ever did tell the truth, then I'd just get happy talk and easy answers. And folks certainly mean well.

Sadly, their realities are not my own.

In the end, I keep my truths to myself and force on a smile instead. "I'm fine. What happened?"

Alec rubs his thumbs across my cheekbones. "You were staring off into space again."

Bry steps up. "I recognize that magic. It made you catatonic."

If anyone would know what happened to me, it would be Elle.

For years, she toted around a magical inhaler to fight something similar.

Alec scans my face carefully. "Did you go back to the forest?"

I nod. "This time, I met a four-horned man."

"Wait." Jacoby approaches our group. "Was he wearing red?"

"Yes," I reply.

Jacoby presses on. "Did he give you a name?"

"He called himself the…" I freeze as a hazy memory becomes clear. Before, I thought the name bandit had meaning. Still, I couldn't figure out what. Now the answer is clear.

"He said he's the bandit, but I suspect he's actually someone else. The Knave of Hearts."

Jacoby pales. "Oh, no."

"Knave of *what?*" asks Knox.

"Don't you know the nursery rhyme?" asks Bry.

"I'm not nursery guy," counters Knox.

Now Agatha joins in and recites the rhyme aloud.

> *The Queen of Hearts*
> *She made some tarts,*
> *All on a summer's day;*
> *The Knave of Hearts*
> *He stole those tarts,*
> *And took them clean away.*

Knox frowns. "So the knave steals stuff and is a bandit. That's it?"

Which is classic Knox. Unless it has fangs and is about to bite your head off, Knox doesn't get the danger.

"It's more than that," explains Jacoby. "The knave is the opposite power to the Queen of Hearts."

"Still not helping," quips Knox.

"It's like this," explains Agatha slowly. "All the mini realms of Faerie align to one of two courts, Unseelie or Seelie."

I can't help but grin. This is Agatha in her *I'm being super patient* mode. It's the one she would use when trying to explain basic stuff around the store, like teaching our stepmother, Marchesa, how to use the cash register.

"I'm Seelie," adds Agatha. She taps her throat for emphasis. "We're lovely but nasty."

Jacoby points to his face. "Unseelie. More openly evil."

"Two courts," says Knox. "Got it. What's that got to do with the Queen of Hearts?"

"In my case, I'm the prince of my own realm," continues Jacoby. "But my lands are vassals to the Unseelie. Still, I rule my own thing. My world is all about the magic of large animals. My family wields Fortitude magic."

"But Jacoby's mini-realm has an opposite," says Agatha. "That's the Miniscule. They control the power inside tiny organisms."

"Like the plague?" asks Bry.

"Exactly," confirms Jacoby. "For the Queen of Hearts, her power is the magic that makes people fall in love. The knave of Hearts holds the opposite power. He breaks couples apart."

Knox tilts his head in a rather wolfy way. "So the knave's the bad guy and the queen is good."

"Not always," adds Agatha. "Some people should never have gotten together in the first place. For them, breaking up is a gift. It depends on *who* wields the power and *what* they want to do with it."

Knox growls. "No offense, but Faerie stuff is a mess."

"It can be," I add.

"So the knave isn't necessarily evil," declares Bry.

"Right," says Jacoby. "He doesn't have to be bad, but this version? Rotten. Word is, he liked to separate people not only from each other, but from life itself. The guy got locked up in a secret prison ages ago. No one knows where."

"Looks like I just solved that mystery," I state. "Someone

chucked him in the ether. Which is pretty clever, except for the fact that the ether is opening up these days. At this rate, the knave will escape soon." I then go on to explain everything the knave said, including his hatred for the Queen of Hearts. Once I'm done, I turn to Alec. "You've been quiet. What do you think?"

Alec straightens his stance. A steely look takes over his blue eyes. "In a matter of days, the Glass Slipper Festival takes place Central Park, which is the queen's realm on Earth. And her magical enemy, the knave, is about to break free and go after everyone the queen cares about, including my girlfriend."

I've seen that expression on Alec before—he's come to a major decision. I take his hands in mine. "What is it?"

"I'm canceling the festival."

All I can do is speak a single word. "Whoa."

16

ALEC

Knox stares at me like I just sprouted a second head.

"What did you say?" he asks.

"The festival is cancelled," I repeat. "Effective immediately." It's a reflex to look over at Elle as I say this last part. "I won't risk anyone's safety."

"Elves like the knave don't go after with humans," explains Jacoby. "If the knave does break free, he'll want to destroy the queen, her territory, and her people… in that order."

I shake my head. "I won't risk fae, either."

Elle steps away. "But we just sold out the event. It's too early to cancel. At the very least, we should check whether the risks are real."

Knox nods. "Bry and I will call up the pack. We can beef up security at the event and run some scenarios on cleaning everyone out of the park."

"Agreed," says Bry. "I bet we can empty out the place in a few hours, tops. That gives you more time to make a final call."

"And I can open a portal to the Faerie Lands right now," adds Jacoby. "Agatha and I will chat up our contacts there. Maybe there's some info about the knave or queen that could give us an edge."

"Good thinking," says Elle. "Whatever's going on, we know who has all the answers: Colonel Mallory the Magnificent. He's a hard fae to find, but it's worth a try."

"Look." I hold up my arms, palms forward. "I get that you're all trying to help, but that answer is still no."

Elle laces her fingers with mine. She turns to address the group. "Everyone, can you excuse me and Alec for a minute?"

In reply, the room erupts into different versions of *yes*. Elle pulls me into the bedroom and shuts the door.

17

ELLE

nce inside Alec's bedroom, I'm happy to find that Hollywood hasn't redesigned anything yet. The place is nothing but concrete walls and steel furniture—the very look that inspired the name, Man Can.

My reasoning here is simple. It'll be hard enough to have this conversation as it is. Not sure I could manage it with a twelve-foot tall version of me looking down over everything.

Alec shoots me his most winning smile. "If you wanted to jump my hot bod, the least you could do is ask first." He blinks at me innocently. "Now, I'm all shy."

"I didn't ask you here to fool around."

Alec sets the back of his hand on his forehead in a pose of mock misery. "Oh, the horror."

It's hard not to laugh, but I somehow manage to keep a straight face. "Alec, I know how important this company is to you. If we don't hold the festival, what will happen to all your employees? Canceling means giving them all pink slips."

Alec sighs. "I know."

"Then there are the dwarves. I haven't known them as long as you, and already, I feel like they're family. If you close down Le Charme, you know what that means."

Alec sits on the edge of his mattress and balances his elbows on his knees. "I must balance the lives of seven dwarves versus the existence of thousands of fae who live in Central Park. Sometimes there are no good choices."

"The Queen of Hearts is no pushover. She probably has a plan to protect her own in case anyone invades. It's not just the knave she has to worry about, you know."

Alec pinches the bridge of his nose. "I can't, Elle."

I sit down beside him. "What's this really about?"

Alec meets my gaze straight on. "You. The knave wants to hurt the woman I love."

"Don't be so modest. You're also a warden. You're probably on his hit list as well."

"It's not the same. I haven't been visiting him in the equivalent of his supernatural jail cell." Alec takes my hands in his. An urgent look shines in his blue eyes. "What if we go away from New York? There are warlock colonies that are far off the grid. You'll be safe there."

"Even from warden magic?"

"I can't stay in the city and wait until the knave decides to attack." He lifts my hand and touches a gentle kiss on my palm. "I can't risk you, Elle."

"Hey, I'm not at any more risk than usual. You should've seen my life growing up with an evil stepmother." I fix Alec with a serious look of my own. "All I'm saying is this. We try, Alec. Please."

Alec stares at me like I just figured out how to stop panty lines, cure cancer, and set up a colony on Mars... all at once. "For you, Elle? Anything."

My heart warms. *That's a really sweet look, right there.*

A knock sounds on the door.

"You coming out, yeah?" It's Knox.

Alec rolls his eyes. "Give us a minute."

But Knox keeps right on talking. "I've been sent here to say we've all decided the festival is gonna happen. Bry and I are checking security. Agatha and Jacoby are doing recon in the Faerie Lands. And Gustav went on a donut run. Says he won't share, neither."

Alec crosses the room and opens the door. Knox stands on the threshold.

"Everyone's left?" asks Alec.

Knox does that one-shoulder shrug move of his. "Sure. We figured it would take a few minutes for you to figure out you can kick anybody's ass, especially some red elf with extra horns. And did we call it?"

I shoot Knox a friendly wave. "You called it."

Alec sets his fist on his hip. "So what do you expect me and Elle to do now?"

"I don't know, man. We'll all be gone for a few days. Take a break. Go play with your gemstones or whatever it is wizards do to relax." Knox raises his pointer finger. "Only don't play Magicorum Killers until I finish my game. I don't trust you not to delete it."

Alec chuckles. "Okay, we'll think of something."

"Good, I'm meeting up with Bry at her place." Knox looks at me. "That is, *your place*. Eh, you know what I mean." Knox turns and saunters off.

Ah, Knox. there's only one.

I rub my neck and think this through. "Our friends are now forming cross-alliances. This might be dangerous."

Before, Alec chuckled. Now he all-out laughs. "Too late."

Which is true. Our friends are nothing if not headstrong. If they want to hang together and make decisions solo, then that's what will happen.

Alec checks his cell. "Since the festival is still on, I have work to do. My people know how to set up any kind of event, but they like to see me hanging around."

I rise from my spot on the mattress. "It's the same with me and the animates."

The festival includes a stage show where models will show off all the new jewelry. Afterward, the animates from Cynder Mercantile will come out and discuss their art. My animates are just as self-sufficient as Alec's folks, but they're also artists. Which means they love it when I show up and say they're awesome.

And if this all works, who knows? Alec and I could end up essentially running Le Charme Jewelers together.

It's a thought that's exciting and terrifying. The scary part comes from the little voice that keeps warning: it's only a matter of time before you ruin it all, Elle Cynder.

And it's true. Some people just aren't meant for happily ever afters.

ELLE

The rest of the day is a blur of chatting up enchanted weavings, carvings, and glass sculptures at Le Charme HQ. All of them are animates, and each one is excited for the Glass Slipper Festival. For his part, Alec chats up everyone from event planners to IT geeks. The guy has a gift for acting as interested in the CFO as he does the kid who prints out name tags.

With every passing moment, more of my heart gets attached to Le Charme Jewelers. I want this to work. When the dwarves stop by to give Alec a huge blue diamond, I even get a little misty. Folks like that give their all and truly deserve the best.

Afterward, Alec is walking me to my apartment. We go over everything that happened. The festival is coming together so smoothly, it's like the event is under an enchantment. It's not fair that this stupid knave could ruin everything.

When we reach my door, I can't help but yawn. "I'll sleep well tonight."

"Same here."

Ever since the dwarves gave Alec the blue diamond, he's been turning it over in his hand. I gesture toward the stone. "Is that rare?"

"Yes." Alec narrows his eyes. "And it makes me think. There may be a spell or two that can help us with the knave. Want to join me in my gem study tomorrow?"

Oh, the gem study. That would be where Alec casts his more complex warlock spells. I've gone in a few times, but I've never seen Alec actually do wizardy stuff in there.

Which means there's only one answer to that question.

"Absolutely."

19

ALEC

For all my talk about being tired, I don't get much sleep. Once I start thinking about creating a new gemstone spell, I can't stop. In fact, it's a serious exercise of personal restraint that I don't wake Elle up at dawn. Somehow, I'm able to push it until 8 a.m.

MagicMan: u ready?

OnlyCallMeElle: on my way

The entrance to my gem study is hidden in my bedroom's far wall. Looking back, I should've connected to the kitchen instead. I like regular snacks when I'm casting. If I stockpile grub in my study, then the food inevitably gets a few magical rock splinters inside. So far, I've chipped two teeth.

Ah, the problems of being a gemstone wizard.

All of which is why Elle and I grab breakfast (or in my case, second breakfast) before heading into the study proper. In some ways, this is a boring block of a room. Everything is made of dark wood. There's no furniture. The walls are lined with tiny drawers.

Elle hangs by the door. "Where should I stand?"

Suddenly, the lack of any chairs seems like a big miss. I've never had anyone else in here while I'm working. Closing my eyes, I picture the spell and stone I need to fix the situation.

As I hone in the gem I need, the walls of the room spin. It's a lot like a casino's slot machine, only instead of tumblers that feature numbers and letters, my room sports panels with tiny drawers.

The walls stop spinning. A drawer slides open on its own. A small chunk of smoky quartz rises into the air before flying over to my hand.

This particular stone is preloaded with a spell. That's what I do here—place magic into stones so I can cast more quickly later on. Closing my fist around the gem, I activate the spell. The stone flares with heat and light. Pale brightness glows through my hand as a leather club chair rises from the wooden floor.

"What do you think?" I ask.

Elle bobs her brows. "That's a mighty cool spell."

I wink. "I haven't even gotten started."

Elle settles onto the chair. "What's the plan?"

"Plan A is the easiest one. We get answers from the colonel. The man's a dragon shifter who's been around since the beginning of Faerie. If anyone knows the real story on the knave, it will be Colonel Mallory the Magnificent."

"And plan B?"

"We deal with that if necessary. Plan B involves creating new magic, which is never stable or advisable."

"So we definitely need to do plan B."

I chuckle. "Plan A first. Time is tight and the colonel's our fastest route to answers."

"True. But I've already tried using summoning incantations

on him, many times. When he doesn't want to be contacted, the guy is a wall."

"Perhaps we just need to knock harder."

Elle sits up straighter. "I'm listening."

"My summoning spells are strong, but I can harness extra power here in my study." Stepping over, I brace my arms along the top of the chair. Long seconds pass as energy rises between me and Elle.

"What if you threw your magic into the mix?" I ask.

Elle tilts her head. "How could I do that?"

"First, I need the right stone." Much as I hate to step away from Elle, it's best to summon stones from the center of the chamber. Once I'm back in the middle of the room, I raise my arm and open my hand.

"Smoky Azure number 74," I call.

I recently loaded this stone with the ability to share magic as well as perform a summoning. In other words, it's the perfect choice for today.

The walls spin again until a new drawer appears. This one is identical to all the others except for the tiny lettering on the outside.

SA-74.

I snap my fingers. The stone rises to zoom through the air and land gently on my palm. Magic zings across my skin. There's a slight chill to the power, which means it's fresh and ready to use.

Perfect.

I refocus on Elle. "Now that I have the stone, it's time for the second step."

"Which is what, exactly?" Elle's eyes are wide with interest. It's a good look on her.

For weeks, Elle's been trying to master her own magic. There hasn't been time to experiment with combining our power.

That changes now.

I cross the room and retake my pose over her. This time, I brace my hands on either side of her head before leaning in closer. "Now, we share magic."

Elle stares at my mouth. "How?"

"Many ways." Inch by inch, I move closer until our lips almost touch. When I speak, my voice is low with need. "But we'll start off easy. Kiss me."

Elle quickly breaks the distance between us. Her mouth caresses mine in a way that's both tentative and hungry. Desire heats my blood. Our kiss deepens. Tasting Elle is so good, I almost forget the purpose here.

Still, I pull on the power of the stone within my grasp. The gem turns icy against my skin as the spell begins. The rock brightens until thin beams of light shine out from between my fingers. The magic's coming into its own now. Power rolls up my arm and into my chest.

Tilting my head, I kiss my way up Elle's neck. Once I reach her ear, I whisper my request. "Will you share magic with me?"

Elle nods.

"I need your words."

"Yes." Elle's voice is husky. "Please."

I draw the stone's power up my throat before touching my mouth to hers once more. If our kiss before was fierce, now it turns even more rough. Our tongues slide. Elle nips my lower lip.

Magic moves between us. Every cell in my body vibrates with energy and need.

"Now speak the incantation," I state.

"I summon you, Colonel Mallory the Magnificent."

We continue to kiss as light surrounds us. A supernatural heat envelops us both.

A familiar voice echoes through the workroom. "Back off, sugar. I'm busy. And tell your boyfriend to keep his hands to himself."

The light dies. We're still kissing.

"Such a shame," I say. "The colonel is not available."

"It really is terrible," states Elle. Little by little, the club chair flattens out into a cot. When it's done moving, Elle lies beneath me.

"Hmm," I say slowly. "I was the one who created the spell for this chair. I don't recall enabling the thing to turn into a bed."

Elle loops her arms around my neck. "Good thing I'm getting better with my magic, eh?" She starts unbuttoning my shirt.

In all my life, I've never been happier that a spell failed.

Thank you, Colonel Mallory, for being so incredibly hard to contact.

And no, I'm not keeping my hands to myself.

ELLE

A blissful hour goes by while Alec and I share each other's bodies and magic. Where has this gem study been all these months? Why haven't Alec and I been hanging out in here, sharing energy and sex all day long?

I'll have to change that.

Which brings things to the present moment. Alec lies behind me as we cuddle like spoons on our little bed. He kisses the top of my ear. "There's still plan B."

"Right. I forgot about that." My sneaky side sparks with interest. "Is this some kind of experimental thing that could kill us?"

"Any chance of death is minor. But the experience will certainly be both unstable and strange."

I wiggle out of Alec's arms and pull my sundress back on. "You know me. That sounds awesome."

Alec winks. "I've noticed." He gets dressed as well. I'd like to say that I'm a lady who doesn't peek at every naked inch of him during the process.

But I can't.

In no time, Alec is ready as well. His shirt's askew and he's not wearing any socks with his loafers. Yet that somehow makes him even more attractive. He moves to stand in the middle of the room.

"What's the Plan B spell?" I ask.

"You know how casters can put their own memories inside of things?"

"Sure, to keep them safe from other people or whatever."

"And you recall how Kir'Adel trapped me inside a gemstone prison."

"Hard to forget." I tap my chin and run through my memories. There are quite a few, considering how I entered Alec's prison myself. "Kir'Adel's jail also contained some of her memories. They were written onto books. Most were pretty boring, but I can see where you're going with this."

Alec strikes one of his male model poses—this selection is where he leans against the wall while kicking his left ankle over the right. "I figure that if you can trap actual people inside of a gem… and if a stone can hold recollections inside… then why can't I trap other people's memories inside a rock?"

"It depends on the magic user," I state. "Many have wards on their recollections. It won't be easy to pull those memories loose."

"Which is why I'll place the spell inside a particularly powerful gem." Alec raises his arm once more. "Bring me Blue Diamond Number Two."

The walls spin around once more. Another box opens and a massive diamond rises up from the container. The thing is as big as an ostrich egg. I recognize it right away.

"That's the stone the dwarves gave you the other day."

"Correct," states Alec. "It should be perfect for this spell." He takes in a shaky breath. Alec is a pretty sunny and easy-going guy, as a rule. A deep and unsure inhale is one of the few ways that I can tell when he's nervous. And I know what helps him in situations like this one.

I shoot him a hearty thumbs up. "Can't wait to see you do your thing."

Alec isn't one for blubbery encouragement. It's best if I keep it light and include a grin.

"Thank you." Alec closes his eyes. "Let the casting begin."

Walls spin. Drawers fly open. Stones zoom through the air in a tornado of movement. In the center of it all, Alec stands like a maestro. He sends some stones toward him and others away. Many gems merge with the massive diamond in his hand. Each time a new gem enters the diamond, the larger stone gets a little smaller.

After a while, the new gems just bounce off the now-tiny diamond. It's taken in all the power it can handle.

"That's it," announces Alec.

Stones fly back into their drawers. The walls cease to spin.

I rise. "How did it go?"

Alec holds the little diamond up to the light. "Doesn't look like the most stable spell ever, but it could work."

I step closer. The blue diamond is literally bouncing across Alec's palm. "That looks unstable, all right." And I speak those words the way some folks might say, *that dessert seems mighty yummy.*

"If we're using this, we have to do it now."

"What will happen?"

"We'll go inside the stone."

"And what'll we find there?" I cross my fingers. "Please tell me you have no idea."

Alec grins his best surfer-guy smile. "Not a clue." He holds extends his free hand toward me. "Ready?"

"Always."

I clasp his palm. Dark smoke fills the room. Energy shifts across our skin. When the haze clears away, the study is gone. Instead, Alec and I stand on the shortest and most unusual patch of street that I've ever seen.

I can only hope that things get weirder from here.

MEMORY GEM

21

ALEC

ot bad, if I do say so myself.

So far, the spell is working perfectly. My study is gone. Instead, Elle and I stand before a line of buildings that are all shaped like books. Beyond the structures, dark mist billows out toward a hidden horizon. The stale scent of old paper hangs in the air. Tiny cobblestones link together beneath our feet.

At this point, some folks might cower and hide. Not Elle. She marches right up to the nearest building and takes a closer look.

"None of these have words on them," she reports. "Except for this one." Elle gestures toward the first book-building in line. She reads the title aloud.

A Woman In Love.

"Not too specific." I report. "Still, with any luck, this could be exactly what we need."

Which is information to keep Elle safe from the knave. Ever since I heard about the knave's plans, a heavy and protective rage has settled into my bones. Now some of that weight lessens.

And another kind of load lightens as well. After I inherited Le

Charme Jewelers, I've carried extra responsibility. Now some of those worries fade. The Glass Slipper Festival is sold out. The new Le Charme line of jewelry could be a success. My employees —not to mention dwarves—might all be safe.

Elle lets out a low whistle. "This is spell is amazing."

My heart swells with pride. "Thank you. I'm rather happy with how it turned out. I've never cast anything like it and—"

The ground rumbles beneath our feet. A wind strikes up out of nowhere. The scent of charcoal fills the air.

"On the other hand," I add. "Maybe this is a super-unstable spell and we should just get on with it."

"Meh. It's still amazing."

"Are you meh-ing me again? That's twice in two days."

"I am Meh Girl. Behold the power of my sass." The ground rumbles once more. Elle doesn't so much as flinch. I've gone on my share of magical missions in the past, mostly with Knox. He's a good adventure buddy, but a little grim. With Elle, everything is fun.

I march up to the first door and grip the handle. "Here we go." I pull the door open with ease.

At this point, I'd expect Elle and I to walk inside the building. That isn't what happens. The structure flips around so the binding faces away from us. The book then opens while moving toward us. Twenty-foot tall pages loom around. Inch by inch, the walls slowly swing shut.

It's a reflex for Elle and me to grasp each other's hands.

The book-building closes.

22

ELLE

For a long moment, everything is darkness. Questions zing through my mind.

When the book-building reopens, what will we see?

Since this is one of the colonel's memories, could there be dragons?

And will snacks be available?

I'm not proud of that last question, but fooling around always makes me hungry.

When the pages open once more, Alec and I no longer stand on the street of book-buildings. Instead, we're on a lovely terrace of pink stones and matching flowers. Behind us, the shadows stretch off into a deeper building.

I step around in slow circle. "Nothing's out of place here, so I'm guessing we're in the Faerie Lands."

"Agreed," states Alec. "If the spell is working, then we shouldn't be able to interact with the past." Alec steps over to a nearby table. Reaching out, he tries to swipe the glass of wine. His hand passes right through the goblet.

I nod. "Looks like the spell is working as intended."

A servant lumbers out—a fae with a man's body and not one,

but two crane heads. He picks up the wine goblet and sets it on a silver tray.

Memories appear. "Jacoby told me about these fae," I announce. "They died out hundreds of years ago." I step closer. "Why are you gone?"

The servant steps away while a new figure saunters onto the terrace. Out on the magical street, Alec and I noticed how this book-building had been titled, *A Woman In Love.*

Now it's clear who's the main character of this book.

The Queen of Hearts has arrived.

QUEEN OF HEARTS

ALEC

The last time I saw the Queen of Hearts, she was helping me and Elle to get together.

Now I catalog every aspect of the queen. In terms of appearances, this ruler hasn't changed. She's still elf-lovely with cocoa skin, brown hair, and a red gown. It's only in her throne room that the queen shows off crimson wings and tresses.

"The queen's eyes," says Elle. "That's the only place where she looks different."

"Fae live for thousands of years. It's common for them to appear young, but have eyes that seem old. So that could be happening to the Queen of Hearts. Still, that's a weary kind of wisdom. This is something different. She seems sad."

"Maybe it's because she's alone. Do you know when she married the king?"

"Sadly, no."

The Queen of Hearts rules the fae who magically hide in Central Park. That's a short walk from where I live. All of a sudden, it seems like a huge miss that I don't know more about this regent and her life. I can't even recall what the king looks like.

The queen turns around to face the darkness in the building beyond the terrace. Suddenly, the tension in her shoulders visibly loosens.

"You're here," whispers the queen.

A man's voice sounds from the shadows. "My love."

The queen holds up her hand, palm forward. "Please stay where you are. I can't say this with you too near."

There's no response from the hidden man. The queen continues.

"We're opposites. I'm Seelie. You're Unseelie. That alone should be too much for us to have a future. But I believe we could work past such things."

"What are you saying?" asks the man.

"When your rage takes over, you're a different person."

"Of course. That's why I need your help."

The queen sighs. "I need a partner, not a project."

A long pause follows. "You've found someone else, haven't you?"

The queen lifts her chin. The next word seems torn from her. "Yes."

When the man next speaks, his voice is lower. "Is it my brother?"

The queen nods. "Your brother is a different kind of Unseelie." She sighs again. "You know what I mean."

"No, I don't." Now the man's voice takes on a dangerous edge. "My weakling little brother? What a joke. He wouldn't know passion if it were written on his forehead. We both know that you'll never be able to quit me."

At last, the man steps out from the shadows. I gasp when I see who is here.

THE KNAVE

24

ELLE

t first, I didn't recognize the man's voice. But that changes when he says, *we both know that you'll never be able to quit me.* Now there's no question who this is.

The knave.

Even so, it's still a shock when the guy walks out from the darkness. He envelops the queen in his arms and kisses her face off.

I can see what's happening here, but I still can't process it. *Who would have thought the Queen of Hearts would fall for the knave?*

The queen breaks the kiss and steps away. "I can't spend my days setting you on the right path. My chosen king supports me as much as I support him. But this?" She gestures between them. "It isn't healthy."

"Healthy," repeats the knave. "What about the health of the Faerie Realm?"

The knave takes out a dagger, crosses the terrace, and sets the blade on the queen's palm. "Kill me."

The queen's eyes widen. "Stop."

The knave wraps the queen's hand around the handle and

then drives the weapon into his own chest. The queen gasps. The knave pulls out the blade.

The queen pats his chest. "You're fine."

"I told you this would happen. Nothing on Earth or Faerie can kill me. You unite things. I destroy. All that holds me back is my love for you. Leave me and I will erase everything." He points to the ground. "Stay."

The queen narrows her eyes. "No one commands a queen."

The ground shakes. The world around us turns into a pair of massive paper walls. The queen, the terrace, and even the knave… all of them become etchings. The book-building reappears and closes around us.

When the book reopens, Alec and I find ourselves back on the cobblestone street once more. Only this time, the wind is far stronger. The ground shimmies in a steady rhythm.

"So that was helpful," says Alec.

"Now we know the queen and the knave were once an item," I recap. "It doesn't explain how the knave ended up in the ether, though."

I point to the second book on the street. Before, only one book-building showed a title. Now a second has one as well. I read the words aloud.

A Story From The Cliff Of Aisling

"That's in the Faerie Lands," says Alec.

I scan the exterior. "There's no door."

"Maybe we have to scale it."

Turns out, climbing isn't necessary. Just as with the first structure, the structure comes alive. The book-building flips over, opens its pages, and closes around us.

Our second journey begins.

25

ALEC

The book opens to reveal a clifftop. The queen stands at the land's edge. Far below, a great fire roars over the countryside. Tears stream down the sovereign's cheeks.

The queen pulls up a sphere of power and tosses it into the flames below. The orb fizzles out before it gets anywhere near the blaze.

A figure stalks up behind her. It's the knave. "Why waste your magic? You can't stop this."

When the queen speaks, her voice is a rough whisper. "Some of my people couldn't escape."

"You mean those two-headed bird men? I'm so upset."

"Why did you do this?" asks the queen. "The land is ruined now. We can't rebuild."

"Because you didn't detect me at your royal wedding. Still, I was there. I watched your ceremony with my brother. And when you committed to him, that's when I made my vow. I no longer wish to destroy all of Faerie. Just everything you love, just as you eviscerated my heart."

The queen shakes her head. "I'll stop you. And this isn't over. I'll build again."

"Where? This ground is now ruined. All other realms in Faerie are taken. You won't start a war for more land." His eyes widen. "Ah, I have it. You'll go to Earth."

She doesn't answer.

"Your silence is a reply in itself," adds the knave. "So you plan to build a hidden world of faerie beauty under the ugliness of humanity? I'll find you there as well."

"Perhaps. Or maybe I'll find you first."

Little by little, the scene turns from real life into a line drawing on a massive page.

All of which means one thing.

This visit to the past is ending.

Unlike our other experiences with this spell, the page walls materialize and vanish at double speed. The trip to the cobblestone street only takes seconds. Sadly, I know exactly why that's happening. My spell is growing even more unstable.

I can only hope our next visit through time is worth the risk.

26

ALEC

The book-walls open around us. This time, the pages show a familiar structure: Belvedere Castle. It's a popular stop with humans who visit Central Park.

The drawing on the page transforms into reality. Elle and I stand at the base of a small hill with the castle looming above us. In some ways, this version of the park appears as it always does. People walk about. The paths are unchanged.

In other ways, everything is far different.

The women here wear full dresses with bustles. The men all sport top hats and fitted suits. Some children skip by while pushing along large wooden circles with sticks.

I turn to Elle. "Are you seeing what I'm seeing?"

"Do you mean all the stuff from the 1800s?"

"That's exactly what I mean."

A pair of horses clip past, pulling a large open buggy behind them.

Elle grins. "How cool is this? We should definitely catch a buggy ride while we're here."

The ground rumbles beneath our feet. For a moment, the view around us changes back into being a drawing once more.

"Or we could hustle and find stuff out before it all vanishes," adds Elle.

I raise my hand. "That has my vote."

A woman's voice carries over the green. "Off with its head!"

Elle and I share a dry look. No need to discuss further. We both know who we must see now.

The Queen of Hearts.

Elle closes her eyes. I've seen her do this move before. It's how she accesses her fae power of second sight. With it, Elle can see the faerie world that's hidden under the human one.

I can do the same thing, only I must use a gem. Reaching into my pocket, I search for the right stone. Fortunately, I have one loaded with fae power for just such an occasion. It's a pink tourmaline and is kept in its own tiny pocket with a zipper. Like anything with fae magic, it's hard to contain.

Pulling out the stone, I clasp the gem tightly in my fist and begin the spell. Within seconds, the world around me shifts. Suddenly, I can see pixies in the trees. Naiads frolic along the paths. A hidden city lurks underneath a nearby pond. And Belvedere Castle transforms into the queen's palace.

Normally, her majesty's residence is a soaring mix of white marble and pointed towers. But this version is under construction. Only the first story has been built up. There's no main gate yet, let alone any guards.

Elle and I walk inside to find the queen standing in what will eventually become statuary hall. Only now, it's a half-finished room with a few marble statues. The queen pauses before one of the stone figures, eyeing up the face.

"I don't like this one, either," announces the queen. "Off with its head."

At least a hundred pixies zoom in from seemingly nowhere. Their tiny bodies surround the statue in a flurry of action and multi-colored wings. Within seconds, they've enveloped the marble head in a web of tiny ropes before flying away and taking the offending noggin with them.

At the same, another troop of pixies bring in a fresh head and set it atop the marble body. The queen taps her chin and scans the new addition.

"This will do," announces the queen. "Thank you very much."

One of the pixies pipes up. "We can't go back to Faerie, can we?"

"No."

Another pixie speaks up next. "But we won't have to run away again. This land be safe, right?"

"Absolutely," declares the queen. "I promise."

All the pixies fly up to the queen, kiss her cheek, and soar away. The regent's eyes fill with a mixture of sadness and joy.

"I never thought about why the queen set up her new realm in Central Park," says Elle. "She's just always been here."

I wrap my arm around Elle's waist. "Now that I know what the queen lost, it makes these lands even more impressive."

"We can't stand by while she loses everything again."

"And we won't."

Both of us are so caught up in our thoughts, neither of us notices the knave creeping up behind the queen. Before we know it, his sword is raised high and he's about to slice open the queen's head.

The thought hits me. *I don't know how she'll survive this.*

At the last moment, the queen spins about. She now holds a shield in her left hand, which she uses to block the knave's blow.

"How dare you come here?" cries the queen.

The knave tries to strike again, but the queen blocks each blow with her shield.

"I told you I'd attack," states the knave. "And there's nothing you can do. Nothing Earth or Faerie can contain me, let alone kill me."

"I know," counters the queen. "That's why I'm sending you somewhere else that's not part of any world." She raises her right hand. A signet ring gleams on her pointer finger. It's a glassy-looking band adorned with the image of the pyramids.

The knave frowns. "And what's that supposed to be? New jewelry to impress me?" As he speaks, he keeps trying to strike the queen. She blocks each attempt.

A flash of light appears on the queen's pointer finger. The glassy ring expands into long sword that's the shape of an obelisk.

I inch closer for a better look. "I know my precious stones. I've never seen anything like this before."

The knave pales. No question about it. This guy knows exactly what the sword can do. "No. You can't."

The queen grins. "You told me too much. I've figured out how to contain you."

The queen moves as if to slice the knave, but she cuts through the ground before him instead. The earth opens up, revealing a familiar stretch of treetops below. Her plan quickly becomes clear.

The queen is opening a portal to the magic forest.

For his part, the knave loses his footing. The world seems to go in slow motion as he falls through the portal and into the forest below. Once the knave is well and gone, the slice in the ground seals back up again. It's as if there never were a portal to another world to begin with.

The queen waves her arm, the sword returns to being a ring.

Suddenly, the image of the queen turns two-dimensional. Page walls reappear before closing in around us. Moments later, Elle and I are back on the street of book-buildings.

Cobblestones heave beneath our feet. Smoke chokes the air. The book-buildings tumble to the ground.

I focus on Elle. "Are you all right?"

"I'm fine! I think we're out of time, though."

"True." I pull Elle into my arms, grip the tiny blue diamond in my fist, and make a solemn request.

Please, let this work.

27

ELLE

Seconds later, I find myself back in Alec's study. I offer him my fist to bump. "That was amazing," I declare.

Alec returns the gesture. "That was also rather close." He opens his hand. The blue diamond is now a small deposit of dust on his palm.

"Hey, at least we know what we need."

"True," says Alec. "We must find another obelisk sword like the one the queen used on the knave. It's something that's not part of Earth or Faerie… and it could kill the knave if necessary."

"Can you cast one?"

"The festival is in days. I can't do it that quickly." Alec tilts his hand, allowing the blue dust to cascade toward the floor. "It took me months to create all the stones that made up this thing."

We share a long look and then speak six words in unison.

"We need to see the queen."

I chuckle. "I've never done that before."

Alec shoots me a sly look. "What? Travel through enchanted books?"

"That, sure. But I meant how we just talked in unison. It's kind of a relationshippy thing."

"Good or bad?"

I tap my chin, as if the response really needs consideration. "Good. Definitely good."

Alec casts a transfer spell so we can reach Central Park, fast. It's strange to see the place in the present day after just experiencing the 1800s. We approach the palace and ask about the queen. The guards say the queen is away and won't return until her birthday two days from now.

Which leaves us without a lead on the obelisk sword, at least for a few days.

Boo.

In the end, Alec and I spent the rest of the day back at his place. Alec casts test-spells for obelisk swords. Meanwhile, I hang in my (now favorite) club chair and surf the MAGICWEB, which is the secret internet for our kind. I'm a wiz when it comes to browsing for supernatural info. Since I now know what we're looking for, I try to turn up any clues on the knave in general and obelisk swords in particular.

My results? Nada. Alec doesn't turn up anything, either. The guy seems pretty calm, but the whole situation is getting on my nerves. I keep feeling like there's some realization I need to find, but it's always just out of my grasp.

Eventually, Alec convinces me to take a break and get some sleep. He even promises to take me to his favorite concentration place tomorrow, saying it will help both of us prepare for our big days with both the Queen of Hearts and the Glass Slipper Festival.

Can't wait.

28

ALEC

The next morning, I wake up to the sound of Knox pounding on my door. And if you've never heard a werewolf knock, it's enough to wake the dead. I'm not even kidding. We once had a necromancer stay over at the apartment. He confirmed it.

"What is it, Knox?"

"I'm making breakfast."

I sit upright. Knox's new breakfast extravaganzas are legendary. And not in a good way. "Great idea." I hop out of bed. "I'll help."

"That's why I'm knocking. I know how your mind works. You're gonna jump into the kitchen and get in my way. The ladies are coming down in five minutes. Keep to yourself and everything will be fine. Oh, and put on some pants, yeah?"

I stifle the urge to groan. "You got it."

A low drumroll of footsteps sounds as Knox stomps back to the kitchen.

Bry and Elle show up five minutes later, just as Knox predicted. They arrive with smiling faces and extra orange juice. In other words, they have no idea what they're in for.

Awful smells roll out from the kitchen. Knox serves up a pile of brownish goo accented by bits of a spatula. Bry and Elle sit at the table and move things around on their plate with forks. When they speak, their voices have a stuffy tone. No question why, either.

They're trying not to breathe through their noses.

I've been through this before, so I catch Elle's attention, point to the floor, and let some flood slip. Combined with a feigned upset stomach, this will give the impression that something Knox cooked has actually been placed in my body.

Elle gets the hint and does the same.

Soon Gustav shows up for his free meal. He nibbles at the floor, makes a loud *ack* noise, and runs back into the wall.

Lucky Gustav.

As for Knox, the man cleans his plate. Maybe something happened to his sense of taste along the way. I make a mental note to check the guy for food hexes later.

Elle's phone buzzes. She checks the screen. "Oh, my. Grayson texted me a video link." She scans the table. "Okay if I put it on?"

We're all too eager for a distraction, so everyone agrees. That is, except for Knox, who just grunts. That's about as agreeable as he gets this time of the morning.

The Lady appears on the tiny phone screen. With a too-bright smile, she promises to live-stream commentary on Glass Slipper Festival. Then the video feed goes dead.

Elle's phone buzzes with an incoming call. "It's Grayson. I'll put it on speaker."

Grayson's voice echoes through the kitchen. "Hello, Elle."

"Hey, Grayson. I'm here with the crew from the Apex caper. That video clip you just sent us. Is it for real?"

"She means it," says Grayson.

"It's Alec," I announce. "Can I tell my people about this? It would be a huge deal for the festival. They'll want to set up extra monitors."

"You can tell them." Something in Grayson's tone sets my nerves on edge.

"Is this a trap?" I ask.

"Not that I can tell," replies Grayson. "The Lady will kick her grandmother in the teeth if she thinks it will attract viewers. The festival has become a thing. I think she just wants in."

"What's the Lady up to right now?" asks Elle.

Good question.

"She's running a livecast," explains Grayson. "Doing that bit she calls, Your Favorite Things. This time, she's trying to summon the object most cherished by the human Queen of England."

Elle lets out a low whistle. "That's a bit rude."

"For the Lady, it's the usual. Her audience loves it." A screechy voice echoes in the background. "Oops, the Lady's calling me. I'll meet up with you at the festival. Gotta run."

The yelling goes silent as Agatha ends the call.

Wow, I don't envy the girl that job.

29

ELLE

Once the breakfast-o-torture is over, we depart the very stinky kitchen and hang out by the massive picture of yours truly. I'm so glad to be away from the stench, I don't even mind having huge-me stare down at regular-me.

After Jacoby and Agatha arrive, we all go through what we've learned over the past few days. Knox and Bry report that with their wolf pack, they can clear out Central Park in two hours, tops. If they can do it as wolves, then they only need ten minutes.

Which is cool. It's a little scary to picture a pack of massive werewolves running through Central Park, but you never know when that ability might come in handy.

For her part, Jacoby reports that the Queen of Hearts is visiting the Faerie Lands until her birthday tomorrow. That tracks with what the guards told me and Alec yesterday. It's just odd, that's all. The queen never leaves Central Park. And after seeing what happened to her homeland in Faerie, I don't blame her.

What could be so important that she'd take off?

Agatha states that she and Jacoby also tried to convince some fae to leave Central Park until the festival is over. No one was interested, to put it nicely.

Then Alec and I share what we've learned. We go through the history of the Queen of Hearts and the knave. It begins with the story of a bad relationship... moves on to how the queen's lands were destroyed... and ends with why the knave is imprisoned in the magic forest. The guy is nearby impossible to imprison or kill.

We try to close on a positive note by saying how the knave can be killed with the queen's obelisk sword. I add how Alec and I plan to visit the regent's palace tomorrow. Agatha and Jacoby volunteer to join us, which is very appreciated.

After that, everyone goes off to do their respective stuff. Bry and Knox want to take the pack on a run in the mountains. Agatha and Jacoby plan to visit Faerie and check on Jacoby's herd.

Which means there's only one thing left to discuss.

I turn to Alec. "What about our special trip today? I wore my new sandals and everything."

Alec winks. "It's still on." He pulls out a gemstone from his pocket.

"Where are we going?"

"It's a surprise."

A swirl of magic appears as Alec transports me to what turns out to be one of the coolest spots ever.

Coney Island.

WONDER
WHEEL
LAND
GON

30

ELLE

The transport spell drops off me and Alec in what looks like a borderline-cheesy fairground. You'd think it's a bad idea to finish a transport spell in the middle of a public place. After all, humans know that magic is fading from the world. They'll shoot a million selfies with anyone who's suspected of being Magicorum, let alone a celebrity like Alec. So I prep myself for an onslaught of paparazzi.

It doesn't happen.

The reason why soon becomes clear. Alec dropped us off behind the Cannoli Dessert Nachos truck. The place gives great cover and smells delicious to boot.

Alec pulls out a baseball cap and sunglasses from the many hidden pockets of his sport coat. He pops them both on and throws his arms wide.

"Welcome to Coney Island!" cries Alec. "Ever been here before?"

"Once I almost ran a con at this place, but the mark fell through at the last second."

"So that's a *no*. Allow me to show you around."

Alec takes my hand and leads me out onto the midway

proper. There are tiny huts with impossible games. I've read about these—you pay way too much money to win massive stuffed animals that tear open on the car ride home. We also pass a carousel that plays tinkling music. And there are tons more food trucks that smell of sugar and grease. My mouth waters just reading the signs.

Deep Fried PB&J

Chicken on a Waffle

World's Largest Pizza Cone

My stomach rubles with joy, and it's not just because of the dining options. As a rule, Alec and I share adventures together. Most of these episodes involve life, death, and some mind-blowing sex. All of which means that the two of us haven't dated in the traditional sense. Sure, I was a fake intern in Alec's company for a while, but I don't really count that as courtship.

Yet today totally counts as a date. There is a destination involved and some fun, selfie-worthy activity. I even wore my cute new sandals which is a total bonus. Everyone knows you have extra powers of attractiveness when you wear something for the first time.

After trying a bunch of bad-for-you foods—my teeth are still buzzing from too much cotton candy—we head over to the main attraction: the Wonder Wheel. The ride's run by an older woman with a crinkly face and a wide smile. The fact that she's shaped a lot like a muffin would've made me hungry ten minutes ago. Her name tag reads Maisie.

When it's our turn to board, Maisie gives Alec the once over.

"My Little Le Sweetie!" she cries.

Alec grins. "I wasn't sure you'd remember me."

"How could I forget?" asks Maisie. She sets her hand at hip level. "You were this tall when you first rode the Wonder Wheel." She turns to me. "And who's this lovely lady?"

Alec pulls me against his side. "Elle."

Maisie winks. "Is she your happily ever after?"

"Yes." Alec kisses my cheek. "She's my everything."

Maisie pulls the wheel to a halt and opens a carriage. Although the thing sits a bunch of people, Maisie only lets me and Alec inside.

"Give me a wave when you're done!" calls Maisie.

The ride begins.

Two long benches line the long walls of the carriage. Alec and I take seats across from each other. The thing creaks and sways as it begins its circuit.

"How do you know Maisie?" I ask.

"My parents used to drop me off here when I was a kid. Maisie would let me ride around the Wonder Wheel for hours." He leans back on the bench. "There's something so soothing about this place."

"And the nickname?"

"I was pint-sized and very smiley. Maisie's always called me her Little Le Sweetie."

I look out through the grating to the midway below.

"What are you thinking?" asks Alec.

"Nothing."

Alec chuckles. "It's a big something, your nothing."

"It's like this. The knave has been saying things to me when I visit the ether."

"And?"

"He believes that some people are poison to everyone around them. I wanted to think I could ignore the guy, but what he said keeps needling me."

"So you're poison? What do you mean?"

"Are you kidding?"

"Example, please."

"To begin with, I'm the only one who still has her fae warden power."

"That's because of the *fae* part of that sentence. It wouldn't be true fae power if it did as expected."

A metal grill covers the window-holes. I run my fingers along the pattern. It's easier than looking at Alec while I say this next bit. "My family fell apart. Maybe the fact that we're together places you at risk, too."

Alec leans forward. "Elle?"

I decide that now's a great time to pick stay chips of paint from the grillwork with my thumbnail. "Huh?"

"Look at me."

Little by little, I shift my gaze to meet his. The expression on Alec's face is the definition of the word *intense.*

"Yes?"

"I only have one dream and you're right here." Alec pats the spot beside him. "Come."

I cross the carriage to sit by Alec's side with my legs across his lap and my head on his shoulder. Together, we watch the world go around. My thoughts turn over what just happened. Alec certainly said some incredibly sweet things. Yet for some reason, none of his sentiments feel real. Because no matter what Alec says, a little voice within me counters.

You are poison, Elle, and all this will end one way: badly.

31

ALEC

I'm not sure how long we ride around in circles, but it's the perfect amount of time. At some point, Elle gestures towards the grillwork that covers the window-holes.

"This pattern reminds me of the work Kokkivo does."

Weeks ago, I wouldn't have known the name Kokkivo. Now I realize he's one of the animates whose creations inspire our newest jewelry line. These days, most animates live in the Le Charme building with the human design team. I even cast enchantments so the two groups could see and work with each other. I worried humans and animates might not get along, but that was unnecessary. The two groups adore each other. If I have to close Le Charme down, I don't know if I'll be able to separate them.

A weight of sadness settles into my bones. Everyone at Le Charme is so excited about the company's future. What if I have to close the doors?

I shake off the thought. This moment is for me and Elle. I refocus on Elle's comment about Kokkivo.

"You mean the Solei line?" I ask.

"That's the one."

I picture the necklaces in question. So many dainty wires twist into a cord of unspeakable beauty. "The layering on those pieces is so unusual. There are many animates in the world. Your parents attracted the best."

A small smile rounds her lips. "Mom and Dad would get so excited about every little creation. The animates soaked that up. The things they made became a way to give back."

I recall what Elle said about being poison to her family. I'd never really asked about them before. Now I wonder what could have happened to make Elle feel responsible.

"What happened to your parents?" I ask.

A long pause follows. At first, I worry that I've pushed Elle too far.

"Mom never seemed sick," Elle finally replies. "Then one day, she was. By the time we got a diagnosis, Mom's body was overrun with cancer. There was nothing we could do. Some things even magic can't fix."

"I'm so sorry." And that's all I say. I want Elle to keep going, but I know how it is with stuff like this. You can't force it.

"Did you know my parents and stepmother all grew up together?" asks Elle.

"That's not a typical part of the fairy tale template."

"It's more common than you'd think. They called themselves the three musketeers. Marchesa always wanted Dad to notice her. My father and mother were a pair from the age of six. Later, when Mom got sick, Marchesa swooped in. Dad was at a low point and Marchesa told him exactly what he wanted to hear. That if they married, Mom's death wouldn't have any impact on me."

"You knew differently."

Elle nods. "I couldn't tell Dad that, though. It was one of the only things that gave him a sense of peace... the idea that I'd be fine. For a long time, I hated Marchesa. And I was so angry at my mother for putting up with her frenemy all those years. Now, it's different. I see that Marchesa was the victim of her own lies, too."

I pull Elle's legs more tightly against my torso. "How so?"

"Life is tough, right? But my mother was always happy. Marchesa believed that joy was because of my father. And it was… in part. But Mom has the right name. Rae. She's simply a sunny person. Bad things happen and she decides to see the good side."

"Like, *the glass isn't half-empty, it's half full?*"

"More like, *wow, the glass is shattered on the floor, but don't the shards sparkle so prettily as they cut our feet open?*"

We share a little laugh. "Rae sounds extraordinary."

"She was. Sadly, Marchesa never understood her."

I shake my head. "What happened when Declan and Marchesa married?"

"I know you'll be shocked." Elle gives me a sly look. "But Marchesa was never happy. My father died of a broken heart and Marchesa took out her anger on me and Agatha. My step-sister is a really good person, by the way. She tried to help me wherever she could." Elle tilts her head. "May I ask you a question now?"

"Sure."

"How was it with your parents? They were Cinderella life templates who met and married at a Glass Slipper Ball. Did they expect each other to make them happy?"

I wince. "That's not easy to answer."

"You don't have to say anything."

"No, I want you to know. It's just that the Cinderella life template is tricky. Everyone knows how the girls have it rough. But guys like me? It isn't easy for us, either. I've looked into hundreds of other so-called Prince Charmings. If your parents are forcing you into choosing a random bride at a ball, then something is definitely wrong in your family."

"Makes sense." Elle kisses my chin. My heart warms.

I continue. "The funny thing is, my parents actually got their happily ever after. Not with each other, though. They were both deeply in love with Le Charme Jewelers."

"How so?"

"The name... the money... the glamour... my parents couldn't get enough. They met as strangers and stayed that way."

Elle frowns. "I don't get it. If they cared that much about the company, then why is it in such rough shape?"

"They treated the company the way they treated themselves. As long as everything *looked* right, it didn't have to *be* right. Does that make sense?"

"It does."

"My father always had these grand schemes, like building the L Center. But those weren't real businesses. It was more fun to have a huge building named after you in the middle of Manhattan." I sigh. "And everyone around them played by the same rules or got fired. I was surrounded by a world of beautiful illusions... and I was the only one who saw the truth."

A memory appears—a young Elle delivering boxes.

I take Elle's hand in mine. "Then I saw you at the L Center's loading dock. You were all things gorgeous and bright. That Rae light from your mother shone all around you."

Elle looks away. "I was a sweaty mess dragging a broken wagon of knickknacks."

I set my knuckle under her chin, guiding her gaze back to mine. "You were perfect in your imperfection. Same as when I saw you later on my security cameras, un-stealing jewelry from my office. For me, Le Charme is a responsibility. It's a broken machine that I inherited and must fix. I'd sell it off if I could, only there's too much debt."

"And too many dwarves."

"Yes, I can never forget the dwarves." I brush my thumb across her lower lip. "But you? You're my dream. And not because you'll magically make everything better, either. It's more that I trust you to my marrow. You'll fight at my side to make our life the best it can be."

"And I love you, too, Alec Le Charme."

We share a slow and loving kiss.

All in all, it's a good day. In fact, our time together is so sweet, I almost forget that we must see the Queen of Hearts tomorrow.

Almost.

32

ELLE

I wake up with a smile on my lips. Alec and I had such a nice time yesterday. After Coney Island, we went back to the city for a carriage ride through Central Park. After all, we missed our chance to have one back in the 1800s.

In fact, I'm so calm, I almost miss how my roomie, Bry, lurks nearby. I yawn, smack my lips, and try to figure things out.

"What's up?" I ask.

"It's happening again," warns Bry. There's no missing the worried look in her eyes.

Instantly, I'm wide awake. My mind races through everything that could be wrong at this point. Top of my list is that the knave is now roaming through our apartment with his machete (or whatever you call that huge sword he has strapped to his back.)

I hop out of bed and grasp Bry by her upper arms. "It's him, isn't it?"

"Yes." She exhales a shaky breath. "Knox."

"Wait." I drop my death grip on her shoulders. "Did you say, Knox?"

Bry frowns. "Who else would I be talking about?"

"I thought the knave was running around with a machete."

"The way you described it, I think he wields a falchion."

That's Bry for you. Information goes in her head and never leaves. I've never even heard of a falchion before.

I jog in place to let off some tension. "This is good. No knave. This is about Knox." I stop running and crack my neck. "Okay, I'm ready now. What's the problem?"

Bry hugs her elbows. "Knox wants to make breakfast again. You know, since it was such a hit last time."

I narrow my eyes and start to scheme. "How long do we have until he comes over?"

"Five minutes." Bry clasps her hands at her waist. "Tell me you've got a plan. I literally barfed yesterday."

"We could tell him he's no chef."

"But you saw how excited he is. The guy spent most of his life running after the people who killed his parents. It really means something to him that he can cook for his new family."

I tap my lips and scheme my ass off. "How attached are you to the kitchen?"

"It's a room full of things," says Bry. "That's it. What are you thinking?"

"I'll summon Gustav and his friends. They can chew through cords and destroy a kitchen in no time."

Bry sighs. "Do you think they'd do that for us?"

"We'll need to buy a bunch of donuts, but yeah. Gustav is the best."

Bry sets out her hand. "Give me your phone. I'll order delivery from the place up the street."

I open my mouth, ready to ask why Bry needs my cell. Then I realize the truth. For this ruse to work, it needs to appear as if I ordered breakfast because I didn't know Knox was coming over.

Wow. Bry is truly developing a sneaky side.

I hand over my cell. "Make sure you get french crullers." Those will play nicely with all the food I ate yesterday at Coney Island.

While Bry types away, I close my eyes and summon my best rodent friend.

Gustav, I need your help.

My little mouse buddy skitters out from under the floorboards. He sits upon his haunches. "What's up?"

"Can you destroy our kitchen appliances right now? It's kind of an emergency."

Gustav blinks up at me with his little button eyes. "Complete wipe out or just chew through the cords?"

"The second thing."

Gustav rubs his little hands over his face. That means he's thinking this through. "I was about to head over to the Apex. I'm picking out a surprise nesting spot for my girl." He shuffles back toward the wall. "Maybe next time."

I flash him my most winning smile. "Bry just ordered donuts for delivery."

Gustav freezes. "Sam's or Nick's?"

Bry flips my phone around to show Gustav the receipt. "Sam's."

"Yes!" Gustav does that thing where he whistles with his pinkies. A dozen mice pour out from the walls and race into the kitchen. Once there, the many creatures zoom under appliances and into a new set of floorboards.

Sometimes, I wonder what the world is like inside the walls of my apartment.

More often, I decide it's best not to know.

Gustav and his crew have just gone to work when the doorbell rings. It's Knox and Alec. Just as Bry predicted, Knox carries two large bags of groceries. Alec is toting a distinct look of panic.

I wrap my arms around Alec's neck and pull him into a big hug. "Don't worry," I whisper.

"How can I not?" Alec shoots a look over to Knox, who is in

the kitchen and safely out of hearing range. "He's cooking again. There are only so many times I can drop food on the floor. I'll have to eat something today."

"Not to worry," I reply. "Gustav is on it."

Alec leans back while narrowing his eyes and pursing his lips. This is what I call his *professor Alec face*. "Really?"

Hand in hand, we march over to the kitchen. Sure enough, Knox is flipping switches on all the appliances. "Nothing's working." Knox crosses the room to turn the overhead lights on and off. "It's not a broken circuit."

Bry shoots me a nervous glance. "What do you think it is, Elle?"

I gasp and point to the bottom of the stove. "Gustav, is that you?"

Now, I stopped trying to have Gustav do things like clean floors or help with laundry ages ago. Mostly, I ask my mouse buddy to perform recon on missions in exchange for donuts. All of which is why Gustav replies without missing a beat.

"I got hungry, Elle."

I sigh. "You're not supposed to eat appliances."

Gustav lifts his chin. "I am a rodent. Chewing stuff is just what I do. Don't put your two-legged perceptions of normalcy on me."

Bry nods. "He has a point."

The doorbell rings. It's the donut delivery, along with Agatha and Jacoby. After we stuff ourselves, we all run through our plans for the day.

Bry and Knox say they promised the pack they'd go on another run in the mountains. Their wolves have been spending lots of time casing out Central Park. To be at their best, the pack needs to run today before tomorrow's Glass Slipper Festival. Which I totally respect.

Alec and I share that we're off to visit the Queen of Hearts, along with Agatha and Jacoby. Today is the queen's birthday.

Based on everything we heard, her royal highness should be back in her palace by now. Hopefully, she'll share some info about the obelisk sword.

As we head out to the park, I feel certain that everything will go well today.

Which normally means stuff will go off the rails and soon.

33

ALEC

After enjoying the best donuts in New York, our crew heads over to Central Park. The place is abuzz with energy as folks get ready for the festival. Scaffolds and workers are everywhere.

A sense of pride spreads across my chest. *Elle and I did this.* We came up with the idea for the new line and now, it's about to happen.

I look to share the moment with Elle. Only she's standing a few yards behind the group. Which wouldn't be a big deal, except Elle's staring off into space. My eyes widen.

Not again.

I step up to Elle. "Are you okay?"

Elle blinks and refocuses on me. "It's all good. I mean, it's actually great! I started to get pulled into the ether again but then… it just stopped."

"That's good." *Which it is.* So why do I feel like there's a hidden problem here?

Elle shrugs. "Who knows? Maybe we won't need that sword from the Queen of Hearts after all. Our warden magic could just be settling in without any more trouble."

I try to force a smile and fail. "Let's hope."

Elle winks. "But along with hoping, we'll also go over to the Queen of Hearts and see about that obelisk sword. I'm a *safety first* kind of gal."

Voices carry through the park, interrupting our chat.

"You must listen to reason." That's Jacoby.

"No, I want Elle." The second speaker is someone I don't recognize.

Elle and I step over. As it turns out, one of Elle's fairy buddies, Nix, is sitting on a bench while glaring hot death at Agatha and Jacoby. Which, in the way of the fae, means that Nix just smiles innocently at them. It takes years of painful experience to tell when a fairy is about to lose it.

Agatha kneels before Nix. "Don't you hate having all these humans around? Why not take off for another part of the city, just for a few days?"

The look on Jacoby's face turns downright pleading. "It's for your own safety."

Nix gestures toward Elle. "I'd like to speak with one of my own kind. A fairy." Nix flashes the rest of us a smile that's both lovely and lethal. "The rest of you can leave now."

Elle gives my hand a gentle squeeze. "It's fine. We'll meet up at the queen's palace."

I kiss her gently on the cheek. "See you there."

As I step away, I can feel Nix's beautifully threatening gaze on my back.

Fairies. Nothing to mess with.

Nix

ELLE

𝒩ix scooches over and pats the spot beside her on the bench. I sit down and wait.

Over the years, Nix has helped me on many capers. Like Gustav, she's great at reconnaissance. Gustav can check out any spot at night; Nix is great at tracking marks across the city during the day. Gustav works for food; Nix does it because she enjoys being naughty. That's the fae for you.

"Prince Jacoby and his Seelie girl keep coming around," declares Nix. "They've talked to all the fae in Central Park." There's an accusation in the way she says those words.

"I know you don't trust elves. Still, I've known Jacoby and Agatha all my life. They're only trying to help."

Nix folds her arms over her chest. "I'm not leaving. I don't care what an elf tells me to do."

"Come on," I state. "You hate humans and the place is over-flowing with them." I fix her with a serious look. "Why not go?"

When Nix speaks again, her voice is barely a whisper. "I've never talked about this before. Did you know I used to be part of the queen's realm back in Faerie?"

"No, I didn't."

"Do you know what happened there?"

"I just found out." I picture the fireball rolling across the land-scape and shiver. "I'm so sorry."

"I lost everything in the knave's fire. Afterward, the land was nothing but tar and dark magic. The realm was ruined. I'll never run away again."

I nibble my lower lip. How much should I tell Nix? In the end, I decide it's best to be honest.

"The knave might return, Nix."

"I'm aware."

"You are?"

"I know my queen better than most. If she's leaving Central Park, it's because of that monster." She forces on a carefree grin. "Don't worry. The rest of the fae are oblivious."

I tilt my head. Nix is an adrenaline and mischief junkie, the same as I am. "What do you plan to do?"

"Nothing." Nix winks. A swirl of silver fairy dust surrounds her. When the sparkles fade, Nix is gone. I try to summon her a few times. Nix ignores me.

In the end, I set thoughts of Nix aside and head off to see the queen. I find Alec, Jacoby, and Agatha standing along the path to the palace.

"Are you waiting for me before trying the gate?" I ask.

"Not exactly," replies Agatha. "We already went to the palace. The Queen of Hearts is in residence today."

Jacoby frowns. "Only, she won't let us in."

"Oh." I smile my face off. "This is the type of situation that I live for."

"Which is why we *are* waiting for you," adds Alec.

I rub my hands together. "One caper, coming up."

35

ALEC

$\mathcal{E}$lle now moves into what I call her *heist pose*. This involves setting all her weight on her right leg, placing her fists on her hips, and scrunching up her mouth. A long moment pauses before she throws up her hands.

"I've got it." Elle turns toward Agatha. "How's your moonlight magic?"

"Depends what you need me to do."

"Know much about a false moon?" asks Elle.

This is an optical illusion where the moon looks larger near the horizon. Human scientists can't agree why it happens.

Hint: it's all caused by fae magic.

Agatha nods. "I know the basics."

"Think you can make something terrifying? We need the guards to look away for a few seconds."

Agatha bobs her head, considering. "I can do that."

Jacoby sets his hand on Agatha's waist. "I've a little magic that can help as well." They share a sweet smile.

Agatha blushes. "Thanks." She looks toward Elle and me. "Get in place near the gate. Jacoby and I will do the rest."

The queen's palace sits on a small hill, the same as the human version. A thin walkway leads over a gulley and into the entrance. The guards protect the main doorways.

Staying low, Elle and I sneak around the back of the palace. With careful movements, we crawl into the gulley and hide under the walkway. The guards above us don't suspect a thing. Once we're in place, we wait.

Inches above our heads, Jacoby and Agatha march across the access bridge. The guards, a man and woman, wear both red armor and irritated frowns.

"We've talked to you already," says the male guard. "The queen isn't seeing visitors today. Move on."

In reply, Agatha summons a sphere of grey magic. It's semi-transparent and gives off a gentle light. As Agatha lowers her hands, the sphere raises into the sky and gets larger.

Then it becomes the moon.

The guards' eyes widen as Agatha's creation expands.

"That's an illusion," says the male guard. "Nothing more."

Still, the pair are so focused on Agatha's moon, they aren't watching Jacoby as closely. The elf prince summons his own sphere of magic and rolls it out across the ground and into the woods beyond.

The guards are distracted, but not entirely so. The female guard points to Jacoby's orb as it rolls away. "We see that," she warns.

"Keep it up and there will be trouble," adds the male guard. "We don't want to fight you." There's a slight wobble in his voice and I don't blame him. Agatha and Jacoby are powerful rulers in their own rights. On one hand, attacking them for playing a prank could start a war. On the other hand, Agatha is powerful enough that her moon could destroy both the guards and half the palace. It's a tough decision... and a distracting one.

Funny the things that come to mind when you're about to sneak into the palace of the Queen of Hearts. One of my hobbies is human magic. It doesn't involve the supernatural. Instead, what humans consider to be magic is really the art of distraction.

And in this moment? Agatha and Jacoby are combining both fae magic with the human distraction.

Agatha's illusion kicks into high gear. Despite the sun, Agatha's creation takes over the sky. Shadows fall over the palace.

"Enough games," says the female guard. "We won't warn you again."

The moon tumbles from the sky and crashes onto the ground. The earth heaves. Trees snap. Agatha's creation rolls toward the palace door. For their part, the guards hold their ground. Still, the two warriors wince as the moon closes in.

That's our cue.

Elle and I crawl up from the side gulley, careful to step onto the bridge behind the guards. Neither of them notices a thing. Moving at top speed, we race into the palace proper.

Behind us, Agatha's moon reaches the edge of the walkway. The guards shiver, but stay at their posts. At the last moment, the moon vanishes. The fae version of Central Park returns to normal. Every tree stands, safe and unharmed.

"Ha!" calls the female guard. "We knew it was a game."

Jacoby turns toward Agatha. "I can't believe they didn't run."

"True." Agatha sighs. "That was one of my best illusions."

"Go home!" cries the male guard.

Agatha and Jacoby trudge off into the forest, careful to keep their shoulders slumped in defeat.

They really are an impressive pair.

Elle and I speed through the reception room and check the main chambers on the building's first floor. We across a few startled servants, but no one else.

It isn't until we reach a back hallway that we run across the Queen of Hearts herself.

She does not look ready for visitors.

QUEEN OF HEARTS

36

ELLE

In some ways, the Queen of Hearts looks as she always does outside her throne room: tall and curvy with cocoa skin, brown hair, and a red velvet gown. There is one big difference, though.

This time, the queen holds a very large sword.

Yipes.

Alec and I stop in place. I force on a smile. "Happy Birthday, your Majesty."

The queen frowns. "I should have known you two would sneak past the guards."

"We must speak to you," explains Alec.

"I'm busy," retorts the queen.

As reactions go, this isn't as bad as it could be. The queen holds a weapon, but she isn't waving it in our direction. Also, the way the queen said those two words—*I'm busy*—carried the tone a mother might use with a naughty child.

"We know about the knave," states Alec.

"And I've been inside the ether," I add.

"I'm aware," says the queen. "The ether first pulled you in four days ago."

I tilt my head. The queen knew about my ether issues? I hadn't considered that before. Although, it does make sense. If the queen can jail the knave in the ether, it makes sense that she'd know if his prison were failing.

Still, the queen could have cast a divining spell to get the same information.

"How could you know I entered the ether?"

When the queen next speaks, she states each word as if it were a sentence all to itself. "Because. I. Am. Me."

The queen raises her sword. The weapon glimmers with magic; then it fades from sight. But before the blade completely vanishes, I catch a flash on the queen's pointer finger.

The glass signet ring.

At this point, I want to cheer something like, *Ha! You knew I got into the ether because of that ring! And even better, we can use that band to create an obelisk sword and take down the knave!*

But I don't.

Years of caper practice come in handy that way.

Instead, look over to Alec. With the barest of motions, I angle my head toward the queen and hope Alec gets my meaning. *Did you see that?*

Alec responds with a subtle nod. *He saw it, all right.*

Today's visit to the palace takes on a new mission. When I did my remote high school classes, I'd often have to finish word math problems. *How many apples can Billy eat before he's done?* That kind of thing. In this case, a new problem appears.

How will Alec and Elle separate the queen from her signet ring?

In such cases, I still find the best plan involves getting others to spill their guts. So I refocus on the queen.

"I'm glad you understand about the ether. You must understand. We're all in danger."

See what I did there? I played a little dumb. Mostly because revealing that I know the queen used to date the knave opens up awkward questions. And at this point? Long discussions about past relationships won't get us any closer to that signet ring.

"What's the danger?" asks the queen smoothly.

Right. She knows the risk. The queen just wants to know if *we're* aware.

"An evil elf is imprisoned inside the ether. He may break loose soon and attack the fae of Central Park."

The queen's features turn unreadable. "Anything else?"

"The Glass Slipper Festival takes place tomorrow night," I add. "It's really important to Alec's company. We need to be sure that the fae are safe… and so is everyone at the festival."

The queen sighs. "My hunting party just slew an entire Grendel horde. In return for our services, we were given magic that seals up the ether forever. Happy birthday to me. Now you can go."

"But what if the ether isn't fully sealed?" I ask. "Is there some way to defeat anyone who escapes?"

"You must have some kind of weapon," adds Alec.

"And assuming you do," I say sweetly. "We're wondering if you would please share it with us? We'll even make a bargain."

There. I said the B-word. Bargain. Fae love that.

On reflex, the queen moves her hand behind her back—it's the same hand that wears the glass signet ring. "I have nothing that could assist."

In other words, she won't share the ring. *Oh, well.*

The queen folds her arms across her chest. "And now, you may leave."

Alec and I share another look. Without speaking a word, we both know what the other's thinking.

We can't walk away when we're so close.

Alec bows. "With all respect, your Majesty, we must stay. There's too much at stake."

"Leave," repeats the queen.

A new voice sounds from behind us. "Come now, my love. They deserve to know more."

Turning around, I see the speaker.

It's the King of Hearts.

KING OF HEARTS

37

ALEC

The king steps closer. He has blond hair, even features, and none of the drop-dead glamour of many royal elves. I like him instantly.

"Please, my love. Tell them the full story. They've been pulled into our mess for no other reason than being born wardens."

I recall the queen and knave kissing on the terrace. While the knave sizzled with passion, this king exudes a calm confidence. I can see why the queen chose her spouse. This man's kindness balances out the queen's fire.

Sure enough, the queen's hard features melt into a smile. "You're right."

The regents move to stand side by side.

"We fae have unusual gifts," begins the queen. "Especially those of us who rule. For my part, I have a unique history and knowledge of the ether. Years ago, the colonel asked me to teach him about it. I sent the old dragon away. More recently, the colonel asked me again. This time he wanted to know where the warden's magic had gone. Once more, I got him to leave."

"I see," says Elle with a grin. "You used fae double-speak to convince the colonel you didn't know anything."

"Correct," states the queen. "Even after your visit to the pyramids, the colonel wasn't aware the ether was an actual realm. This suited my purposes at the time. You see, I didn't want anyone interfering with the ether."

The king gestures toward Elle. "You may have met a four-horned man there."

"Yes, I did."

"He's my brother," says the king. "The Knave of Hearts. Indeed, we royals gain special powers. For my brother, nothing in Faerie or Earth can hurt him. It's impossible to even contain him. My brother also wields a horrible temper; he can become a different person when enraged. Something had to be done to keep the queen safe."

Something had to be done to keep the queen safe? That's an understatement. The knave burned down the queen's entire realm. That's what you call borderline psychotic.

"In the end, I found a solution," says the queen. "I imprisoned the knave in the ether. A family relic assisted me." Here the queen absently rubs her invisible signet ring. "Then you wardens released so much magic, the knave's prison was compromised."

"We didn't realize that would happen," Elle explains.

"I'm aware," states the queen. "If I could do it over again, I'd tell the colonel everything from the start. This whole nightmare might have been avoided."

The king wraps his arm around the queen's shoulder. "That's all in the past," he continues. "What's important now is how the ether's been at risk. The queen's relic can open and close the ether, but not fix the situation of so much warden magic making it unstable. To fix the situation, we needed allies."

"I knew the colonel would aid me," adds the queen. "Which he did. You don't need to worry about the ether anymore. We've siphoned off enough to keep it stable."

"So you've removed some ether," I recap. "How can we know that'll work?"

"Allow me to show you," says the queen. "I call this the Ether's Key."

She pulls out a small vial from her pocket. My brows lift. I've seen bottles like those before.

ETHER'S KEY

38

ALEC

"That's a genie bottle," says Elle.

"True," agrees the queen. "The colonel called in a personal favor and approached one of the djinns."

"Let me guess," says Elle. "Skye helped you." She's Elle's friend and a bit of a softie when it comes to aiding others. *Not a common trait among the fae.*

"That's right," confirms the King. "Skye gave us a genie bottle for containing the ether."

The vial wobbles in the queen's grasp. "It doesn't like being trapped," she reports. "So if it ever did get loose again, it would be even more unstable."

"One day, we'll set it free," says the King. "Nothing should be contained against its will, even magic."

"And you're certain it's safe?" asks Elle.

"This vial always stays on my person." The queen resets the bottle into her pocket. "Nothing could be more secure."

The queen's words rattle around the back of my head. There's a warning them, but I can't quite place what it could be.

Elle still stares at the vial like it's a stick of dynamite instead of a supernatural lockbox. "How can we know that's really working?"

"A fair question," says the queen. "About twenty minutes ago, the ether called you. The summons failed. Am I correct?"

Elle nods. "How did you know?"

The queen raises the bottle once more. "At the time, this container glowed blue. Over time, it will become even more efficient at blocking the ether."

"And now, you understand," says the King. "And there's no need to worry anymore. This matter with my brother is *our* responsibility. The queen and I have taken care of it. Doesn't that put your minds at ease?"

The king looks at us expectantly. Clearly, he's waiting for us to agree that everything is fine. Elle and I don't say a word.

"Know this," adds the queen. "Bringing the two of you together was a product of my magic. I unite souls. And I protect the love I forge."

"We won't allow anything bad to happen to either of you," adds the king. He's rapidly becoming my favorite elf (after Jacoby and Agatha, of course).

"Thank you." Elle shifts her weight from foot to foot.

"But?" prompts the queen.

"I don't know." Elle huffs out a shaky breath. "It's just… we normally have a lot more drama in situations like this."

The queen smiles. "Maybe this time, you'll simply have more laughter. Not every encounter is trouble. It's not like your life is poisoned."

Elle forces a grin. "Maybe not."

"Now." The queen claps. "You must return to your normal lives." She wags her pointer ginger. "Only be sure to save me a piece of cake tomorrow. After all, today's my birthday."

Elle shoots me a questioning look. "What do you say? This is your call, Alec."

I set my hands in my pockets and rock on my heels. This is a huge decision. So much has happened in the past few minutes. I must ensure I'm not missing anything.

The queen pins me with a pointed stare. "You *will* hold the festival tomorrow, won't you?"

I run through everything one last time. The Ether's Key... the werewolf pack protecting Central Park... and the signet ring. I'd feel better if we had the signet ring, but there's still time for Elle and I to figure that out. Even without it, there's enough for me to give the queen an answer.

"Yes," I state.

I exchange a quick look with Elle. There's no need for us to share a long conversation. Both of us know what we still must do.

Get the queen's signet ring.

An idea appears. I clear my throat. "I'm no good at speeches. Still, I wish to take this moment to thank you for watching over me and Elle. I suspect you've helped out many people such as ourselves. Few of us have the chance to express our appreciation. Allow me to speak for everyone you've united when I say, thank you. "

The queen's eyes glisten. "You're very welcome."

Elle rushes to envelop the queen in a big hug. "Thanks so much."

The queen pats Elle's shoulders. "Enough of that. Go enjoy the festival."

I grin. "We will."

After shaking hands with the king, Elle and I march out of the palace at a brisk pace. Once we're safely outside, I whisper to Elle.

"Did you get it?" I ask.

Elle winks. "Easy peasy. I started slipping rings from fingers when I was eight."

I exhale. "Perfect. Now the queen has the troublesome ether contained... *and* we have a way to fight the knave even if he escapes."

"So the festival really is on?" asks Elle.

"Oh, yes," I reply. "One hundred percent."

GLASS SLIPPER FESTIVAL

ELLE

It's really here. The Glass Slipper Festival.

The event has barely begun and already the Great Lawn in Central Park is packed with people. A massive stage fills one end of the long and rectangular space. Kiosks, food trucks, and tents line the periphery. Above them, massive screens hang from metal frames.

The red carpet is set up on the other short end of the rectangle. Although the sun has gone down a while ago, this area shines like midday. Cameras flash as everybody who's anybody strolls down the red carpet and into the Festival. Or rather, they speed into a nearby VIP tent.

Alec and I watch from the sidelines. We haven't made our entrance yet, and I'm trying to look calm about that fact. Bry, Agatha, and I spent hours today getting ready. Even with all the support, I still feel exposed and underdressed.

Which is simply not logical. It's just that I'd be much more confident in disguise right now. A gorilla costume would be ideal. Or a plumber's onesie. I'd even wear one of my FBI uniforms. Hey, I'm not picky.

For his part, Alec sports his classic jeans, sport coat, and calm

CEO vibe. It's his casual stance—combined with his sunglasses and baseball cap—that makes everyone wonder, *is that really Alec Le Charme?*

I re-smooth my already-perfect dress. It's a fitted sheath of crimson silk. When I saw it in the store, I thought it was 70's retro and hot. Of course, now it seems like every chick here is wearing red.

Stay cool, Elle. You can wear your gorilla costume when you get home. Strangely enough, that thought really helps.

Alec steps into my line of vision, interrupting my self-worry fiesta. He slowly eyes me from head to foot. "You're almost perfect."

I do a double-take. "Almost?"

Alec reaches into his sport coat and pulls out a long velvet box that's a distinct shade of purple.

I shake my head. "Alec, you don't need to do this."

"As a matter of fact, I do." He opens the jewelry box to show off a ruby necklace. Three lines of small red stones loop and twist about each other. It's a design that we prototyped but didn't have time to complete.

"It's beautiful."

"And the gems also hold a protection charm." Alec takes out the necklace and sets it around my throat. "I cast the spells myself."

"Protection?" I give Alec the side-eye. "What do you think is going to happen?" I hold up my right hand and twiddle my fingers. Although no one can see the band, both Alec and I know the truth: I still wearing the glass signet ring.

"A wise woman once told me, *enjoy the best… but plan for the worst.*"

I grin. "Hey, that woman was me."

Alec takes off his sunglasses. "I've no reason to doubt the Queen of Hearts. And you are wearing the glass signet ring. Still, we've always been honest with each other. You've got to know I'm anxious about tonight."

"It's a big deal, what with the company and all."

"Hey, I didn't give the company an extra necklace." Every line of Alec's face pulls tight with intensity. "I know you can take care of yourself. Still out of everyone here, I'll always be most concerned about you."

I brush my fingers across the jewels around my throat. I've spent so many years on my own. Some nights, I wondered if anyone would notice if I just disappeared. Alec's sentiment is just as precious as this necklace.

"Thank you," I say, my voice rough. And I kiss him.

ALEC

I soak in the sight of Elle in her red necklace. The jewels aren't as beautiful as my woman, but they're close.

From our hiding spot in the back of the crowds, we watch the flow of celebrities on the red carpet. Elle and I have a few minutes to kill before it's our turn. I pull up my cell and run through a quick checklist.

General festival stuff?

Running like a charm, from cameras to models to everything in between.

Animates?

Hanging backstage with Agatha and Jacoby.

The Lady?

On standby with the IT guys. I still can't believe she's keeping her word and co-hosting the stage show via remote. Maybe Grayson is right—the Lady can't pass up a chance for some spotlight.

Knox and Bry?

While in human form, their pack discretely polices the park. Knox keeps sending me angry texts about how people aren't where they should be. Bry says to ignore him, so I do.

Before us, the red carpet empties out of the last few celebs. A sense of anticipation hangs in the air. That's our cue.

I look to Elle. "Ready to walk the red carpet?"

She cracks her neck. "So ready. I've decided to treat this as another caper." With two fingers, she gestures between her eyes and the crowd. "I'm fooling them all into thinking I'm Queen of Romania."

"I think you could pull it off."

Setting my hand on the base of her spine, I lead Elle to the red carpet entrance. I've been doing this since I was a kid, so walking and waving doesn't seem like a big deal to me. But Elle takes it on like an art form. Cameras flash. Reporters ask for comments. Elle and I wave, smile, and walk.

It's glorious.

Once we're done, I'm thrilled to see the flush of excitement in my woman's eyes.

"How was it?" I ask.

"A rush!" She grins. "We'll have to do that again soon. I can pick a new country each time."

I chuckle. "I love that idea. Ready to head backstage? The show's about to begin."

Elle beams with delight. "Let's do it."

And in this moment, anything seems possible. Perhaps Elle and I can usher in a new age for Le Charme and ourselves.

As my woman said a few days ago, it's all worth a try.

41

ELLE

After the red carpet fiesta, Alec and I head to the performance. In short order, we're waiting in the wings. The stage itself is long and rectangular. Towering monitor panels line the back wall and serve as a high-tech curtain. Right now, all the screens show a single message: "Welcome to the Glass Slipper Festival!"

While we wait for the show to start, Alec chats up his team. I can see why he's so obsessed with helping these people keep their jobs. They're hella efficient and smiley. Sometimes, the company seems more like a happy cult of bejeweled hippies than a global capitalist powerhouse.

A single worry keeps pricking at the back of my mind. Grayson. She hasn't texted me about when she'll arrive at the festival. Still, I'm sure she'll show up eventually. Grayson's not the type to promise and bail.

I tiptoe up to the edge of the curtain and peer out into the crowd. My thought is to find Grayson, but one thing becomes instantly clear. There's no chance I'll see any individual faces. From this high up on stage, the lawn is nothing but a sea of people that stretch off to the horizon. It's more like a rock concert than a fashion event.

For a moment, I just soak in the wonder of this moment. Alec steps up to my side.

"We did it," he whispers.

I shoot him a sly look. "Almost."

Music strikes up and Alec saunters out on stage. With every step, the man simply exudes energy and charisma. The hover cameras fly about him, grabbing the best angles. The screen bank behind shows images of Le Charme fashions through the ages.

I can't believe it. This is real.

Alec slaps on his best surfer-boy smile. "Good evening and welcome to the first Glass Slipper Festival!"

A roar of approval erupts from the crowd.

"I'm Alec, CEO of Le Charme Jewelers. Tonight, we'll introduce our new line of affordable and fashionable adornments for everyone. You'll see our first new collection in more than one hundred years!"

Another round of cheers follows.

"Afterward, we have a special treat for you. This collection is inspired by the work of magical objects called animates. Thanks to some enchanted cameras, you'll get to see these supernatural animates as they really appear to those of us in the Magicorum… and you'll also meet the animates' leader, Elle Cynder."

I grip the curtain more tightly. People don't know me as well as they do Alec. *Will anyone be excited that I'm part of the show?*

The crowd cheers again and it's the loudest roar yet. Some of the worry seeps from my bones. At least, the audience likes the idea of me. That's a start.

Alec raises his arms. "But there's more. The lovely Lady R has agreed to share her live commentary."

A familiar image takes over the wall of screens behind Alec. It's the Lady. At this point, the crowd loses their collective minds.

The cheering becomes deafening. Squares of light cut through the deepening night as folks lift up their cells.

"Thank you for the warm welcome," says the Lady. The audience quiets. "I'd like to kick things off with one of my most popular segments… Your Favorite Things! As most of you know, this is where I cast a little spell and see what's hot—and not—out there in the world. Tonight, my magic will answer a question… What item does Alec Le Charme most value now?"

A thread of unease winds through me. This isn't what the Lady said she'd do tonight. Still, what's the worst that can happen?

On-screen, red light reflects from the Lady's cupped hands. Even though it isn't logical, I go up on tiptoe to see what she holds. It doesn't work, of course. The Lady shoots the audience a knowing look.

"What do you think it is, people?"

Folks yell out so many answers at once, it's impossible to hear any single suggestion.

"The easy money is that it's a phone," adds the Lady.

A memory appears. The Lady did this same trick back at the Apex Towers. That time, she really did summon Alec's cell.

Now the Lady raises her hands so everyone can see what she holds. My stomach sinks.

It isn't a phone.

The Lady frowns while pushes the fuzzy object toward the camera. "This seems to be some kind of container."

At first, the image is only a blur. Forever seems to eke by as the cameras focus on what the Lady now clasps. When I see it, every corner of my soul chills over with worry.

She holds the Ether's Key.

The Lady slowly turns the vial so the cameras can get all angles. There's no question about it. This is the exact same vial that the Queen of Hearts showed us yesterday.

"Get a close look at this one, viewers. I bet it's part of tonight's new line of goodies." She parts her hands. There's a crash offscreen as the vial tumbles to the floor.

The world seems to stop.

She did not just do that.

"What shame," says the Lady, although she doesn't seem disappointed in the least. "I dropped it."

I cross my fingers and hope for the best. Maybe the vial is fine. The thing looked pretty sturdy when we saw it at the palace.

After leaning over, the Lady brings the container back up to the cameras. "Ah, everything appears to be fine. What a relief." She holds the vial beside her face, like she's in a commercial for hand soap. "Am I right, Alec? Is this item another part of the new Le Charme line? Did I expose a secret too early? Perhaps I ruined your day unexpectedly?"

Ugh. She really is enjoying this too much.

"No," says Alec smoothly. "It's not part of the current collection. Perhaps another year."

"It is rather lovely, though." The Lady launches into a speech where she shares how excited she is to see the real collection, but I can't hear a word. Instead, all my focus stays locked on the Ether's Key.

A crack runs along the front of the glass. Even worse, a thin wisp of blue mist twists out from the surface. That must be some of the ether.

Panic zings through my nervous system. Still, I force myself to stay calm.

Chill out, Elle. This is nothing to worry about.

After all, what will a little puff of smoke do? It can't be enough to set the knave loose.

Suddenly, the screens turn off. Park lights flicker and die. Everything plunges into darkness. My breath catches.

Lady R, what have you done?

42

ALEC

The Lady wanted revenge for our caper at the Apex, so she dropped the vial. It cracked. Now the lights have gone out. This leaves me standing in the middle of a darkened stage, waiting for all the electronics to come back to life.

They don't.

The crowd grumbles, but no one sounds too worried. I take that as a good sign. Surely, the IT folks will get everything working again and soon. This must be a strange glitch, nothing more.

Boom! Boom! Boom!

Great claps of thunder shatter the night air. A line of lightning arcs onto the stage. Only this bolt isn't just a flash. It hangs in place.

Next, it widens.

Through the bright electricity, I view another world. The realization hits me with the power of a fist. *This isn't lightning, it's a portal.* Through this makeshift window, I see trees towering off into the distance. Which means this isn't any gateway, either. It's the magic forest. Before, only Elle could see this place. Now I can make out every detail.

Then he steps through. The Knave of Hearts. The fiend appears just as he did in the memory gem: a seven-foot-tall Goliath in red robes. Every inch of him exudes pure rage.

The knave extends his right arm. A sphere of power appears on his palm. Adrenaline spikes through me as I realize the truth. *He's casting something.* I reach into my pocket and pull out a gemstone I use for fireball attacks.

The knave is too quick for a counter-spell.

Fast as a heartbeat, the orb of magic stretches out into a magic staff. I brace myself, waiting for a strike. Yet the knave doesn't attack. Instead, he uses his new weapon to spear the stage floor.

Concentric circles of red mist and power move out from the staff, reminding me of the waves made by dropping a large stone in a still pond. This magic rolls across Central Park. As the energy touches each human, they freeze in place. Then, one by one, they vanish.

Elle had described seeing this happen outside the Apex. Still, it's one thing to imagine people dematerializing before you. It's another to actually see it happen.

I inspect the staff more closely. It pulses with energy right where the sharp end touches the stage. The casting is powerful, but simple. If I can pull that staff free from the stage floor, then the human audience will return to Central Park. Assuming I can get rid of the knave in the meantime, no one may ever know he appeared. I can simply claim a lightning strike and power outage before continuing with the show.

Once the humans are gone, the fae of Central Park glow with red light. Hundreds of pixies shine out from their hiding places on tree branches. Water naiads send out crimson brightness from under their lake homes. More red light leaks out from under rocks, which is where trolls undoubtedly hide. My heart sinks.

It's just as Jacoby said—the knave doesn't see humans as anything but obstacles to his revenge. So he's removed them. Now his spell pinpoints those the knave wishes to destroy.

With the fae glowing, the knave tilts his head back and lets out a roar of pure fury. Branches rattle. Leaves fall. Tiny fae weep, a sound that's like the tinkling of sad little bells. I recall how the queen said the knave transforms when he's in a temper.

She wasn't kidding.

A moment later, the knave no longer resembles an elf royal in fine robes. Instead, he becomes a pale demon with fire in his eyes and heavy armor around his entire body. The knave kneels. A wall of flame erupts behind him, sending a blazing panel into the skies.

The humans are gone, so they don't see this display. But the fae of Central Park watch in horror. They take to the skies and race away across the now-empty greens.

"Run all you want," says the knave. "You won't get far." He adds a final statement with extra malice. "I have another quarry to kill before hunting you all down."

THE KNAVE

ELLE

*E*verything happens so quickly, I can't take it all in. It begins when the Lady breaks the Ether's key... then the knave appears and makes the crowd vanish... and finally, the nearby fae glow with red lights that essentially read 'kill me here.'

My mind remains a blank of shock as one of those gleaming fae leaps on stage and flies toward the knave at top speed. It's a fairy the size of a girl with butterfly-style wings. A small dagger is gripped tightly in her right hand.

My dream-like haze deepens as I see who it is.

Nix.

"Leave my queen alone!" Nix swoops her blade toward the knave's throat.

In a single swift movement, the knave runs Nix through with his sword. Then he flicks his wrist to toss her offstage. The look on the warrior's face is the same one I might have when swatting a bug.

More than anything else, it's the knave's expression that snaps me out of my stupor. Rage heats my veins. How dare the knave end Nix's life at all, let alone with such casual malice?

Closing my eyes, I focus on the magic within me. My warden

power crackles inside my soul. Next, I focus on the glass signet ring. The band responds to my warden power. I sense that it's ready to become the sword I need when the time is right.

Only I won't make the same mistake Nix did. Her death has taught me something. I'll sneak on stage and only reveal the obelisk sword when I absolutely need it.

I nod once, the plan made.

I rush onstage.

Some part of me is aware of Agatha and Jacoby running behind me, begging me to stop. I sense Bry, Knox, and their pack racing toward the stage.

They want to help. But I know what must be done. I saw how the Queen of Hearts put the knave into his prison in the first place. I can do it again.

Beside the knave, Alec stands strong and ready. He isn't casting spells or telling me to run away. Like so many times before, he knows my plan at the same moment I create it. Despite the fear and sorrow in his eyes, he raises his fist high and urges me on.

"Do it, Elle."

I rush up to the knave. The demon eyes me with the same disinterest that he gave to Nix, all while fingering the hilt of his blade. At the last possible moment, I summon the obelisk sword and slice the ground before him.

What happens next is just what I saw with the Queen of Hearts. The wooden stage falls away beneath the knave, revealing the magic forest below. An electric sense of triumph moves through me.

It's all going to plan.

Then, it isn't.

The queen attacked the knave on solid ground; I stand on a flimsy stage. As the knave careens through the floor, more wooden slats give way.

The knave falls through to another realm.

I tumble down right behind him.

ALEC

When I first saw Elle run onstage, I could have cheered.

Both of us saw how the Queen used the obelisk sword in the past. And Elle was going in for the same kind of sneak attack. Only before, the queen struck the knave on solid ground. This is a hollow stage. How could I have been so stupid?

Elle has fallen through to the magic forest. The obelisk sword tumbled through with her. Now the stage is back to normal, only with a few loose wooden slats.

I start issuing orders, rapid-fire. "Agatha and Jacoby, try to open a portal to the ether. Knox and Bry, send your pack to the palace. Drag the queen out, if necessary."

Everyone gets to work, myself included. For my part, I try to summon the queen or the colonel using a spell. Those two came up with the vial in the first place. There must be something else they can do now for Elle.

Precious minutes tick by. None of the spells works. Knox and Bry return quickly with news from their pack. I'm pulling for it to be good.

"I tried to explain in my texts," begins Knox. "People aren't where they should be. Another patrol just checked the queen's palace. She's gone."

My stomach drops to my toes. "That can't be right."

Knox sets his hand on my shoulder. "You have to face the truth. The Queen of Hearts may have run off."

"I can't say I blame her," adds Bry. "We all know her history with the knave."

Agatha and Jacoby approach. "We can't keep trying the same portal spells over and over," says Jacoby. "They aren't working."

Agatha nods. "Plus, casting them is using up all the power we might need for something that really *could* help."

I pound my leg in frustration. "Why did I let Elle take the signet ring? If I had it, I could have summoned the obelisk sword. I'd be the one in the magic forest right now."

"You don't have any warden magic," says Jacoby. "I doubt it wouldn't have worked for you. Not without lots of extra magic, anyway."

I shake my head. "Then I should have just kept it myself. Elle wouldn't be alone with that monster."

"None of us had any idea she'd fall through the stage," says Knox. "Stop blaming yourself."

I take a deep breath. "I'll try." Saying those words reminds me of Elle. Hope sparks in my heart.

"What should we do next?" asks Agatha.

"I don't know yet," I reply. "But there must be something. I won't lose Elle."

ELLE

It feels like I tumble forever before landing on the ground. All the air's knocked from my lungs and my dress is shredded. Still, I've kept my grip on the obelisk sword. That's got to count for something.

With wobbly movements, I rise to stand again. The knave waits nearby in his mega armor. The guy doesn't even seem winded.

In this moment, I have limited choices. Namely, I can fight or flee. I am so going with door number two.

I slice the obelisk blade through the air, trying to open another portal that would lead back to Central Park. Or anywhere on Earth, really. I can be flexible here.

Yet no matter how many times I swipe the blade, but nothing magical happens. I tap into my inner power. There's no energy at all inside me. All my fae, enchanter, and warden energy is gone.

A foul taste creeps into my mouth as a memory appears. The last time I visited the magic forest, I tried casting a bunch of spells. I couldn't do anything then, either. The knave said supernatural powers don't work here. At the time, I didn't really care because that lack-o-magic was keeping the knave in his secret prison.

Now, I do care, deeply. My big plan was to use the obelisk sword to flee. Damn.

The knave races toward me. Sadly, he's still looking mighty demon-like in his new armor with his massive sword raised high.

Oh, well. The obelisk sword isn't magical enough to open a portal, but it's still a blade from the ether. Based on what the knave said, this might be the only weapon that can actually kill the guy.

One way to find out.

The knave brings down his heavy sword. I block the blow with my smaller blade. And I am fighting like a boss for all of two seconds.

Before my blade snaps in two.

Next, the knave punches me in the stomach. Hard. It's a total dick move, and it works really well.

I gasp for breath while the knave kicks aside what's left of my obelisk sword. My back slams onto the ground as the knave tackles me. He sets all his weight on my torso while his hands wrap around my throat.

The thought strikes me that Alec gave me a necklace of protection and even that won't help here.

The knave's fingers tighten over my windpipe. My lungs burn for air. And he decides that now is a great time to get chatty because, *of course, he does.*

"Such a shame you came alone," declares the demon-knave. "I've had years to booby trap every inch of this forest. The queen left me here to protect myself from so many monsters. I would have loved to use my creations on your friends. But they'll still suffer, won't they?" He leans in closer as he says his last bit of nastiness.

"Because you're poison, Elle Cynder, and you know it."

46

ALEC

I've speed-cast through every spell I can think of. The only stones left in my pockets are now actual rocks. Agatha and Jacoby have been extreme-casting, too. Nothing has worked. The pair look exhausted.

We're out of options.

The night turns silent and solemn.

"I remember Elle," says Bry quietly. "She was my best friend."

"She smelled good and made Alec happy," adds Knox.

Agatha sniffles. "Growing up, Elle always smiled, no matter what."

Jacoby's voice breaks as he adds his thoughts into the mix. "Elle was my first friend."

Everyone looks to me. Clearly, they want me to add my elegy. That's not happening.

"What are you, crazy? We can't give up. There must be something. We just have to stay alert and think."

The park lies covered in what normally passes for nighttime in New York. Now true darkness falls over us. Something is casting a massive shadow over Central Park.

And I have a pretty good idea who it might be.

I cup my hand by my mouth. "We're over here, colonel!"

47

ELLE

*E*very inch of my body screams for air. I thrash under the knave, but it's no use. The guy weighs a ton. My ears ring. Spots form in my vision.

Not long now.

I've been in close calls before. Still, this is the first time scenes from my life actually flash through my mind. I picture my parents swaying in sync as they stock shelves in our family store. *I Got You, Babe* plays on the loudspeakers. Next, I recall hanging with Bry. We wear matching pajamas while eating our weight in bad-for-you ice cream. The next memory isn't an image so much as a feeling. Warmth spreads through my chest as I share my very first kiss with Alec.

Although my mind isn't ready to die, my body stops fighting. My peripheral vision collapses into a tunnel. How I wish I look upon Alec now. Instead, all I can see are the fiery red eyes of the demon-knave.

"Wish you could cast a spell, don't you?" The demon-knave's voice sounds tinny and far away. "Your magic will never work here."

Suddenly, Alec is here. I must be having hallucinations

because I can clearly see my boyfriend pull down a nearby branch and slam it onto the demon-knave's head.

Whack!

Alec glares at the demon-knave. "Physics works everywhere, asshole."

Pressure lifts from my chest as the demon-knave falls over, unconscious. I pull in rough gasps of air.

Alec crouches beside me. "Elle, are you all right?"

I'm too busy breathing to try and speak, so I simply nod in reply. Inside, I brace myself for the inevitable. Here's where Alec realizes that I'm poison. Being with me means a lifetime of knaves and tree branches, of loss and misery. Now is when it all breaks apart.

Only it doesn't.

I'd declare that Alec grins at this point, but that's like describing the sun as warm. Alec beams. He's jubilant. Waves of pure adoration radiate out from the deepest parts of his soul. Alec's affection connects to hidden places within me. Links form. Possibilities open. A realization begins to take shape. Something new moves closer, and yet it's still out of reach.

I catch my breath. "Thank you, Alec. I'm all better now."

And I mean it.

48

ALEC

When the colonel landed in Central Park as a dragon, I finally saw a chance to save Elle. And the fact that the King and Queen of Hearts also arrived? That made prospects so much better. Between the three of them, they figured out how to allow me to follow Elle into the magic forest.

Once I arrived, I found Elle being choked by the demon-knave. Grabbing the branch and knocking him out was more of a reflex than a well thought-out plan. Still, it all ended with Elle breathing. That's what matters.

Speaking of Elle, her focus snaps to something just over my shoulder. Rustling sounds behind me. I lower my voice to barely a whisper.

"He's coming, isn't he?" I ask.

No question who 'he' is. The demon-knave.

Elle nods.

I meant what I said about grabbing that branch. It wasn't a super-advanced scheme. The demon-knave was hurting Elle; I took him down. That's not to say I didn't have *any* plan.

All of which is why I pull the broken obelisk sword from my

waistband. I picked the thing up when I first landed. It wasn't as satisfying as a branch to the head, but now? As weapons go, this thing is looking pretty good.

Lifting the blade, I set the hilt onto Elle's hands. The thing is more of a dagger now, but hopefully, it's still enough of a weapon to get the job done.

Elle grips the handle and nods slightly. She's totally on board.

I feel more than hear the demon-knave approach. One thing I'll say for the guy; he's certainly stealthy. For her part, Elle keeps her gaze locked with mine. A single glance in the wrong direction could give everything away.

Heat curls up my back as I sense the demon-knave drawing closer…

Closer…

"Now!" cries Elle.

I shift to the side as Elle swings her blade upward. It tears right through the demon-knave's armor as if the stuff were made of paper. The weapon lodges deep in his chest. The demon-knave moans and falls over. I check his pulse.

"He's gone," I declare.

At those words, the ground below us opens up. Elle and I tumble through the earth and land in Central Park. The colonel stands over us in all his Clark Gable-looking glory.

"There you are," drawls the colonel.

The Queen of Hearts steps closer. "You killed him, didn't you?"

"I told you, sugar," explains the colonel. "They wouldn't be able to come back if they hadn't done the job."

The queen keeps her gaze fixed on me and Elle. "I need to hear the words."

"He's gone," says Elle.

"Thank you," states the queen. A mixture of relief and sorrow twists across her lovely features. The king wraps his arm about his wife's shoulder as they march back toward their palace.

"Now." The colonel rubs his palms together. "When I came here, someone told tall tales about a celebration. Y'all better hop to it now."

49

ELLE

The colonel wants the festival back. We're only too happy to deliver. Turns out, the demon-knave's staff still remains jammed into the stage. After Alec removes it, the crowd returns, and a very plausible excuse is given about flash storms and glitchy equipment. The crowd buys every word.

The show is back on.

For her part, the Lady pretends another goldfish met an early demise. She tries to bag on us again, but Grayson arrives with some 'best of' clips. Every so often, we pop up the Lady saying something is phenomenal, and no one is ever the wiser. I worry that Grayson will get in trouble when the festival is over, but she insists there's a plan.

I certainly hope that's true.

The animates become a huge hit. I think some of them may start their own livecasts. And the new jewelry line? It's even more popular. The fashion show ends in a blur of activity and high spirits. Someone pumps tunes through the loudspeakers. Knox, Bry, and their pack take their humans forms and dance. Agatha and Jacoby find Nix—she was injured, not killed—and heal her up with magic. As a result, the fairies of Central Park decide that my stepsister and her boyfriend are honorary members of the queen's realm. They all take to hanging in trees and singing. It's a very fae thing to do.

As the party winds down, I pull Alec aside for a walk in the quieter parts of park. As we step along, my thoughts turn back to the moment Alec saved my life in the magic forest. In the moment, a realization stayed just out of reach. Now that revelation appears to me in perfect clarity.

"You're rather silent," says Alec. "Something on your mind?"

I nod. "Back in the magic forest, I thought I might die. You saved me. Afterward, I saw your face and it all led to this…" I scan the nearby trees, hoping the right word might appear. It doesn't. "It's hard to explain."

"Take your time," says Alec.

We stop under an arch of trees. "You've told me how much I mean to you," I begin. "I knew it yet never fully felt it. But in the woods? I finally discovered the truth. You don't care if I can be poison in your life. You love me through any pain."

Alec wraps his arms around my waist. "Don't forget. I bring my own set of trouble, too. This isn't about living an ideal life. It's about facing things together. I don't care what happens, so long as it's you and me."

A soul-deep kind of love envelops my heart. "I understand that now—" I tap my chest "—in here."

"Then nothing else matters." Alec's smile becomes as bright as it appeared back in the woods. "Kiss me."

So I do.

—The End—

~

The adventure continues with the story of Grayson in TOWERS AND TITHES, Book 8 of the Fairy Tales of the Magicorum

THE KISS

TOWERS AND TITHES
FAIRY TALES OF THE MAGICORUM #8

DESCRIPTION - TOWERS AND TITHES

The adventure continues with TOWERS AND TITHES, Fairy Tales of the Magicorum #7!

About TOWERS AND TITHES

I'm a Tower Tithe with a Rapunzel problem. That's not as weird as it sounds.

Ever wonder how Rapunzel survives without leaving her home? After all, someone must stock groceries, buy hair products and fix the plumbing. Witches don't wield toilet brushes, so "Rapunzel care" becomes the job of Tower Tithes like me. Not that we choose this gig. We're just unlucky elves who get magically chucked into servitude. Since our kind live for ages, being a Tower Tithe can drag on for thousands of years... and I'm eighteen. Yipes.

That said, it wouldn't be too awful if I had a cool Rapunzel. No such luck.

I serve none other than Lady R, the social media sensation and sadist who lives in Manhattan's famous Apex Towers. With the help of her manager—a witch named Jocasta—Lady R releases daily gossip videos while assigning me "torture chores." Many tasks are designed to remind me how Lady R is the gorgeous variety of elf, while I'm beyond plain. I spend a lot of time scheming my escape.

My work pays off when an eccentric billionaire offers to magically set me free. The catch? I must move to Arizona and become his personal assistant. Needless to say, I rush for the door. Turns out, my new employer is none other than Lady R's ex-boyfriend, Dex, a guy who was blinded in a strange accident and has since become a recluse.

In other words, I ran from my fairy tale life, but it found me again anyway.

At this point, I should head for the hills, yet I simply can't leave Dex. For the first time, I truly feel comfortable around someone. In all honesty, it's probably because I have self-esteem issues and Dex can't see my bland face. Even so, it's all good until Lady R discovers where I am. And that leads to my Rapunzel problem.

With Lady R back in the picture, can I still find my happily ever after? The truth will emerge soon enough.

Because my name is Grayson Eyre, and this is my story.

Ideal for readers who crave a mash-up between Rapunzel and Jane Eyre.

~

Fairy Tales of the Magicorum
Modern fairy tales with sass, action, and romance
   1. Wolves and Roses
   2. Moonlight and Midtown
   3. Shifters and Glyphs

LOVE AND ETHER
FAIRY TALES OF THE MAGICORUM #9

BONUS ILLUSTRATIONS

This edition of FAIRIES AND FROSTING includes some extra images and commentary because sometimes, we all need secret cool stuff.

This first image shows one of my favorite views of New York city at night. I worked in Midtown and always felt so welcomed by the energy of the city. It truly has a magic all its own, which is why I've set this series there.

NEW YORK

Much of the story's action takes place in Central Park. It's hard to describe how amazing it is to find a stretch of green space in such a huge metropolis, so I wanted to include this image. In the end, I couldn't find a spot to add it in where it didn't slow down the story. I'm a bit of a nut job about keeping up my pacing!

Central Park

THE KNAVE

This image shows the Knave brooding in his prison. The pose is great—this is someone who's waiting for their chance to return! That said, there were already images of the Knave in the book. In the end, this pic turned out to be another one that just kept slowing down the story, no matter where I placed it. Now it has a home at last!

Knave

FADING ELLE

Originally, Elle would fade away from New York when she went into the Ether. It's a cool idea, but it was just too much happening with the obelisks breaking through the ground at the same time. It's a thin line between just enough and too much action!

In the end, I needed those obelisks in order to hint where the magic really came from. Meanwhile, Elle fading away was more a cool flourish than anything else. So *fading Elle* got cut from this story. Perhaps there will be a home for this concept in another book!

ELLE

*H*ow much do I love this image of Gustav? A whole lot, I can tell you. Sadly, the watercolor style didn't fit with the other images in the book, so I had to leave it on my virtual *cutting room floor*.

GUSTAV

Here's a full body view of the King of Hearts. The artist put a lot of work into the armor and stance, both of which are very cool. However, I decided that it was more important to show a closer image of his gentle expression versus the full body view. But you can enjoy the look now!

KING OF HEARTS

ALSO BY CHRISTINA BAUER

PIXIELAND DIARIES tells the story of sassy pixie Calla and 'her' elf prince, Dare.

Medieval mages ... Slow-burn love ... And heart-pounding action! Check out the BEHOLDER series!

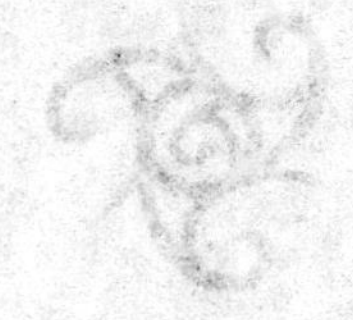

It's been one month, three days, and six hours since I last 'got my gladiator on' and battled in the Arena. Not that I'm obsessing or anything. Sure, I can sneak in and watch someone else fight, but that's a snore.

I roll over on my dingy bed, scooch under the drab covers, and watch the gray drizzle outside my window. Mondays are the pits.

Mom's voice echoes into my bedroom. "Time to get up! You don't want to be late for school, do you, honey?"

I roll my eyes. *Of course*, I want to be late for school.

Raising my head, I open my mouth to say just that, and then decide against it. Instead, I bite my lower lip, yank the pillow over my head and groan. Loudly.

"Don't make noises at me, young lady." Mom rustles papers in the kitchen. "I've a letter right here. You're on something called the Official Watch List for Unreasonable Tardiness." Her footsteps echo down the hall and pause outside my room. "You'll be suspended from high school at this rate. What do you think about *that?*"

I peep out from under my pillow. Mom looms in my doorway,

her fist set on her hip. She's a quasi-demon like me, so she resembles a lovely human with a curvy figure, amber skin, chocolate-brown eyes, and chestnut hair that falls in waves over her shoulders. All quasis have a tail; Mom and I both sport the long and pointed variety. The big differences between us are laugh lines, some grey hair and our opinion of what's 'dangerous' for eighteen-year olds.

I fluff the pillow and slide it under my noggin. Being suspended means no school. Maybe even catching a few Arena matches on the sly. I wag my eyebrows. "And suspension would be bad because?"

"I'd make it that way."

Ugh. She would, too.

Off go my covers. "This is me getting up."

"Good." Mom stomps away.

I shower, pull on some sweats, and sleepwalk into the kitchen, seeing the familiar lime-green appliances, mismatched furniture, and peeling linoleum tile. Everything looks peaceful, quiet, and empty. Another typical Monday morning before another average day at school. *BO-ring*. I'll have to charm Walker into taking me to the Arena later. Until I'm called to fight again, it's better than nothing.

A thick white envelope sits at the center of the kitchen table. I scoop up and read: "To the Quasi-Demon, Miss Myla Lewis, 666 Dante Row, Purgatory." I lick my thumb and run it over the loopy calligraphy. *Real ink*. My long black tail flicks in a nervous rhythm.

Frowning, I tap the unopened letter against my palm. No one sends me fancy stuff like this. In a blur of motion, my tail darts across my torso, grips the envelope with its arrowhead-shaped end, and tries pulling it from my fingers.

"Hey now!" My tail's always had a mind of its own. For some reason, it's decided this letter is dangerous. I jerk the envelope out of reach, but not before one corner gets totally shredded.

"Now, look what you did." My tail slinks behind me to curl guiltily about my ankle.

I reread the outside of the letter. Nothing here to worry about. I *am* a quasi-demon (mostly human with a little demon DNA). I've spent all eighteen years of my life in Purgatory (where human souls get judged for Heaven or Hell, aka the most boring place in the history of ever). This letter's like dozens of others that hit our doorstep each week. Why's my tail on a mission to trash this thing?

I stare at the words again, feeling like they should read: "Open this to turn your life upside-down and your heart into mush."

Clearly, I'm having an off-morning.

I slip the envelope-slash-time-bomb into my mangy backpack. I'll read it later at school.

Mom steps into the kitchen. "How's my sweet baby, Myla-la?" Yes, I'm eighteen years old and Mom still uses pet names from when I was three.

"I'm good." I open a cabinet and pull down a box of Frankenberry cereal.

Mom eyes my every movement, her forehead creasing with worry.

"Did you sleep well last night, Myla?"

Oh, no. Here it comes. I square my shoulders and mentally prepare my 'I'm so very-very caaaaaaalm' voice. "Absolutely." *Nailed it.*

"Any bad dreams?"

"Nope." The 'calm voice' isn't working so well this time.

"Hmm." She taps her cheek. "Met anyone lately? Made any new friends?"

I grit my teeth. All my mornings start off with maternal interrogations like this one. I find it's best to give soothing, one-word answers. "Negative."

"No friends at all?"

"Only the same one since first grade." I raise my spoon for emphasis. "Cissy."

"That's good." She offers me a shaky grin. "You're safe."

I shoot her a hearty thumbs-up. Today's cross-examination ended relatively quickly; maybe Mom's getting less overprotective. A grin tugs at the corner of my mouth.

"More than safe." I speed-chop the air, karate-style. "I'm a lean, mean, Arena-fighting machine." Wincing, I freeze mid-chop. *How could I be so dumb?* Mom loses her freaking mind whenever I say the word 'Arena.'

There's a pause that lasts a million years while Mom stares at me, her face unreadable. Finally, she moves. But, instead of jumping around in hysterics, she flips about and rifles through cabinets in search of a coffee mug.

Wait a second.

This morning Mom cut her interrogation short *and* she didn't panic when I said the word 'Arena.' I wind my lips into an even-wider grin. Sweeeet. Things *could* be changing, after all.

Leaning back in my chair, I watch Mom pour coffee. I know she goes overboard because it's just me, her, and this nasty gray ranch house. I have no brothers, sisters, or straight answers about who my father is, except that he's some kind of diplomat. Add it all up and Mom's a wee bit clingy.

Or, at least, she *used* to be. I drum my fingers on the Formica. A less overprotective Mom opens up all sorts of possibilities. I could watch more matches. I could fight in more matches. I could develop interests in things other than the Arena.

Eh, maybe it's a 'no' on that last thing.

Mom slides into the chair across from mine, her large brown eyes watching me through the wisps of steam curling from her mug. "Want a ride to school today? I don't mind waiting outside the door." A muscle twitches at the corner of her eye. "You know, in case anything happens."

My heart sinks to my toes. Then again, maybe Mom's worse than ever.

"Uhhhh." My mouth falls so far open, some Frankenberry rolls off my tongue and onto the tabletop. Did she *really* offer to stand outside school all day long 'in case anything happens?' Cissy told me how parents get extra-twitchy during senior year. A shiver rattles my spine. My Mom *plus* 'extra-twitchy' *equals* a huge nightmare.

I force a few deep breaths. "Thanks for the offer." It's getting really hard to keep my 'calm voice' handy. "I'll pass this time."

Suddenly, the air crackles with energy. A black hole seven feet high and four feet wide appears in the center of the kitchen.

Out of the void steps a ghoul.

My fingers twiddle in his direction. "Hey, Walker." Technically, he's named WKR-7, but I've called him Walker for as long as I can remember.

"Good morning." Walker nods his skull-like head. If he were a few inches taller, the movement would knock his cranium through ceiling, and he's on the short side for a ghoul. It's a mystery how Walker and the rest of the undeadlies handle an eternity of being so crazy-tall.

Walker pulls back his low-hanging hood, showing pale, almost colorless skin and a strong bone structure. He sports the same hairstyle from the day he died: a brush cut with sideburns and no beard. Great black eyes peep at me from deep sockets.

I grin. It's nice to have Walker around. Most ghouls are obsessed with rules and act irritating as Hell. But Walker? He pushes boundaries like a pro, especially when it comes to sneaking me into the Arena. Having him around is like having a cute and somewhat sneaky older brother, only one without a pulse.

"Be careful, Myla." Walker's thin lips droop into a frown. "That's no way to greet your overlords. I don't mind, but other ghouls could send you to a re-education camp."

I roll my eyes. Purgatory is one massive bureaucracy with the charm of suburbia and the fun of a minimum-security prison. All the work's done by unpaid quasis like me (we're not allowed to call ourselves 'prisoners'). Ghouls keep us in line and make sure we're—*cough, cough*—super happy in our service.

I'm ready to complain about all this to Walker for the millionth time when Mom pipes into the conversation.

"Greetings, my beloved overlord." She's laying it on thick to make up for my sloppy hello. "Want some decaf?" She bows.

Walker nods; ghouls love java.

Mom picks up one of Walker's loopy sleeves, rubbing the fabric between her fingertips. "This is a little threadbare. Are you here for a new one?" All quasis must perform a service; Mom sews and mends robes. It could be worse. My friend Cissy's mom is a ghoul proctologist.

"No, thank you." Walker eyes the coffee pot greedily.

Mom hands him a full mug marked 'Afterlife's Greatest Ghoul.' Her chocolate eyes nervously scan his face. "What service do you require then?"

Walker frowns. "Myla must battle in the Arena today."

A huge grin spreads across my face. When human souls reach Purgatory, they're given a choice: trial by jury, or trial by combat. Based on the result, they end up either happily floating around Heaven or having their souls consumed in Hell. If the human selects a trial by jury, then it's someone else's problem. But if they choose combat—and the combatant in question is totally evil—then someone like Walker ends up in the kitchen of someone like me. I'm one of a few dozen quasis who kick butt. Literally.

I jump to my feet and clear off my bowl. "Now, this is what I call a Happy Monday."

Mom steps back. "You're sending Myla off to fight today? You can't." She leans against the countertop for support. "Every time she goes, she risks her life." A muscle twitches by her mouth. "Those battles are *to the death*."

I stifle a moan. Mom always focuses on the whole 'to the death' thing like it's the first time she's learned how matches work. Hell, I've battled in the Arena since I was twelve and have yet to get a scratch. You'd think the drama would tone down over the years.

Panting, Mom points to a tattered calendar by the door. "My little one fought a month ago. She serves once every *three* months, right?"

I raise my hand. "It's not a problem. I'm up for this. Totally."

Mom flashes me a desperate look. "I know that." She grips the countertop like she'll pull it out of the wall. "Please, Walker, tell me it's a mistake."

Walker's black eyes fill with understanding. "Myla must serve today. There's a spike in Arena matches; all fighters have extra battles."

Mom stares at Walker, her jaw grinding out silent rebuttals. After a few moments, she presses her palms to her face, a low sigh escaping her lips. I frown. She's hitting a new level of drama this morning.

Walker shoots me the barest wink. I fight the urge to smile, knowing it means one thing: there's no across-the-boards spike in Arena matches. Purgatory must have an uber-evil soul on their hands, the worst of the absolute worst, and they need their best fighter on it.

That would be me.

Mom shakes her head from side to side. "All those demons and angels. Promise me, you'll keep her away from 'danger.'" She puts special emphasis on the word 'danger.'

"I always do, Camilla."

Mom releases her death-grip from the counter. "Of course."

My back teeth lock. Mom's always going on about protecting me from angels and demons. The demons I understand, but *angels*? Come on.

I zip up my gray hoodie. "Time to trash some evildoers." Stepping to Walker's side, I wait for transport to the Arena.

Mom's hand lightly touches her throat. "Be safe!"

"I'll be super-safe, don't you worry."

"And don't be late for school."

I slap on a smile. "On it, Mom."

Walker bows his head. "Stand back, I'll summon a portal." A new black hole appears in the center of the kitchen. I glance into the darkness, feeling the Frankenberry in my belly come up for a repeat performance. Using a portal feels like tumbling through empty space with a killer case of the stomach flu. Helpful safety tip: hold a ghoul's hand or you'll fall forever.

Taking a deep breath, I grab Walker's chilly fingers so tightly, I'd cut off his blood flow, if he had any. Together, we step into the portal, topple through nothingness, and walk out again onto the sandy earth of the Arena floor. I try my best to look ready-for-battle instead of ready-to-puke.

Walker offers me a sympathetic glance. "Shall we find a place to sit?"

"Nah, I'm fine, thanks." I scan the open-air stadium around me. The Arena's a nasty old ruin, all chipped gray rock and busted sandstone columns. How the place stays upright is a total mystery. The fighting floor is one huge uneven clod of dirt, the bleachers are basically rubble, and the entire top level looks ready to collapse.

I freaking love it here.

The stands lie open and empty, except for a few quasis. They're all fighters like me, trying to catch someone else's match. Mom used to attend too, but all the moaning and gasping got so out of hand, she was banned ages ago. I can't say I was bummed. Nothing like having your Mom yell 'Baby, don't diiiiiiiiiiiiiiiiie' when you're twelve and fighting a demon for the first time.

A gravelly voice echoes through the air. "Greetings, *slave.*" The word 'slave' is said with particular venom.

Every muscle in my body goes on alert. I'd know that voice anywhere, and I absolutely loathe its owner. I scrape lint from under my fingernails and pretend not to notice the seven-foot tall ghoul looming behind me.

Walker steps between us. "Greetings, SKE-12."

My mouth winds into a mischievous grin. "Hey, Sharkie.'" SKE-12 hates his nickname, so I work it into every encounter.

Sharkie frowns. "My name is SKE-12, *slave.*"

Walker sets his hand on my shoulder, gently guiding me so I stand face-to-navel with Sharkie, master of Arena ceremonies and all-around dickhead. He hasn't changed a bit since my last match, not that ghouls often do. He's gray-skinned with large coal-black eyes, a skull-like hole for a nose, and teeth that have been filed to tiny points. His long silver robes hang in tatters; a tall black staff is gripped in his bony hand.

Walker gives my shoulder a squeeze. "Myla was just about to greet her ghoul overlord properly, weren't you, Myla?" Standing next to Sharkie, even Walker looks vertically challenged.

"My bad." I bow extra-low. "Greetings, SKE-12."

His buggy black eyes narrow into slits. Sharkie always knows when I'm making fun of him, and it drives him crazy. "I'll have no mischief from you today."

I bow again, even lower this time. "Yes, I'm fresh out."

Sharkie turns to Walker, his black eyes flaring bright red. "Control her." His gaze swings back to me. "We've an especially evil human soul fighting today. I hope to watch you die at last."

I pick something off my molar with my pinky. "I'm sure you do."

Sharkie steps closer, his pointy teeth click-clacking as he speaks. "The soul you fight today is so evil, the angels have begged the Great Scala to stand by, ready to transport him to Hell the moment he's defeated. Which will never happen." He leans in closer. "You. Are. Doomed."

My brows pop up. Normally, the Scala migrates tons of souls

at once in what's called an iconigration. For this guy to get solo treatment, he must be a SUPER nasty. *Fun.* "Bring it on, Shar–."

Walker grabs my elbow. "Look, Myla! Your friends are here!" He points across the stadium floor. "We must depart." He bows once more to Sharkie. "Excuse us." As we speed-walk away, Walker whispers in my ear. "If I weren't already dead, I'd have had a heart attack just now."

"Eh, Sharkie's harmless."

"Because I placate him for you." He shoots me a sly look. "Why must you always taunt him?"

"Not sure." I shrug. "It's a hobby." A few yards ahead stands a ghoul named XP-22, and a hovering green blob that's Sheila, the Limus demon.

I shoot Sheila a friendly wave. "Hey Shiel, how are the kids?" Sheila's nice, so long as you don't stand close enough for her to swallow you whole. XP-22, on the other hand, is a total drip. I don't even glance in his direction.

"The kids are good, Myla, getting bigger every day...Just like you." Sheila's entire body shivers, which is a little scary since she's six feet tall, three feet wide, and has fourteen red eyes the size of tennis balls. "It seems like yesterday you were twelve and about to fight your first demon." Her huge gaping mouth twists into a grin. "How old are you now, honey?"

"Eighteen."

A blob-like arm stretches out from Sheila's side, lengthening into a gooey hand with eighteen long fingers. "Almost grown up! Have you been assigned your service yet?" 'Assigning your service' is ghoul-speak for locking a quasi into a life-long job after high school. We're not allowed to call it 'prison labor.' I shiver. There are some mighty foul careers out there too, like the infamous anal probe development lab.

Before I can reply to Sheila's question, Sharkie thumps his staff against the ground.

"Attention!" Sharkie raises his arms, his ragged gray robes

swaying in slow, ghostly motions. Beneath his huge hood, his eyes shine as two points of red light.

Sheila waves her eighteen-fingered hand in my direction. "Well, what'll your service be? Port-a-Potty Squad? Greeter at Ghoul-Mart?"

Pointing to Sharkie, I make a 'sh' face to Sheila. It's rude to talk once the ceremony starts, plus I hate answering the whole 'what'll your service be' question. Sheila nods and oozes away. Bonus.

THUD. THUD. THUD. THUD. Sharkie thumps his staff four more times. "I bring you the Oligarchy!"

Four ghouls in scarlet robes appear along the top tier of the stadium, one at each point of the compass. Called the Oligarchy, they rule Purgatory as one collective mind, and a not-so-creative mind too, based on how they name ghouls.

In one motion, the Oligarchy close their eyes, bow their gray heads, and open a series of massive portals around the lip of the stadium. Angels and demons appear in the dark openings, and then stream down the uneven stone steps in one great wave.

The angels take their seats in an orderly line, their bodies coming in many shapes, sizes and colors. All have massive white wings, floor-length linen robes, little open-toed sandals, and eyes that glow with an unearthly blue light. They can hide their wings if they want to, but they keep them out for important occasions, like watching Arena fights.

In other words, angels are cool.

On the other side of the stadium, the demons move in a frenzied pack, roaring in a mad rush for the best seats. Large, furry creatures stomp along next to small and slimy monsters. Tiny, spiked demons zoom above their heads. Eye color is all they share in common: black stands for 'neutral' while red means 'run for the hills.'

As I watch them scramble over each other, my head shakes

from side to side. Demons are cool too, but only when I get to kill them.

The lively hum of stadium chatter collapses into anxious silence.

She is coming.

I scan the top level of the Arena. The four great portals stand empty and dark. Acting in unison, the Oligarchy ghouls lower their heads. A low hum fills the air. Pale yellow light glimmers in the eastern portal; all eyes turn in that direction. A figure in white appears in the darkened entryway. My breath catches.

This is Verus, Queen of the Angels.

She stands willowy and tall with long black hair, high cheekbones, and exotic, almond-shaped eyes. She's timeless, beautiful, and more than a little bit frightening. Sometimes she watches me so carefully during matches, it gives me the creeps.

Beside her stands a short-ish ghoul with a handsome face, square jaw, and large black eyes.

I elbow Walker in the ribs. "That guy could be your brother."

He looks up, smiles. "You don't say."

"I did say." I glance at him out of my right eye. "So, is he?"

"You know your mother doesn't allow me to share personal information." He shoots me a sympathetic smile. "Take it up with her later." He clears his throat and rocks a bit on his heels. "When I'm not around, if you don't mind."

My 'why don't you tell me anything' fights with Mom are nothing short of legend. I stick out my tongue at Walker. "Fine. I will."

Verus steps onto her balcony, a small entourage behind her. As she slips into a white stone throne, the stadium's silence is ripped apart by howls and screeches. A new outline appears in the western portal: Armageddon, the King of Hell. He's tall and lanky with black onyx skin that's smooth as polished stone. A blade-like nose divides his long face, ending in a pointed chin. He scans the stadium, his eyes blazing as two searing points of scarlet light. A shiny black tuxedo hugs his wiry frame.

Unholy Hell. Every nerve ending in my body goes on alert. While Verus is a wee bit scary, Armageddon gives off a 'greater demon' aura. If you get too close (which has happened to me more than once), every cell in your body shudders with terror. But that's not what *really* gets me about the King of Hell. Most demons are short-term thinkers. They want to kill your body and eat your soul, end of story. Not Armageddon. He planned for years to take over both Hell and Purgatory. That kind of craftiness brings evil to a new level.

Armageddon saunters away from the portal, a large entourage of gorilla-like Manus demons behind him. The Oligarchy collapse onto their knees as he passes by, their movements reminding me of marionettes whose strings are cut. Their deep voices echo through the stadium. "We praise thee, Great King." The ghouls may rule us in name, but everyone knows who *really* runs the show.

Without so much as a glance toward the Oligarchy, Armageddon speeds onto the balcony across from Verus, his entourage close behind him. The King of Hell slips into his own black stone throne.

Sharkie thumps his staff again. "Ghouls, demons, and angels!" The stadium falls silent.

I glance at my watch and grin. Right now, I should be in homeroom.

With a flourish of his bony arm, Sharkie gestures to the four scarlet-robed ghouls standing along the stadium's top level. "Today, the Oligarchy bring you a spectacle of governing efficiency: an Arena battle to the death witnessed by the magnificent leader of our joint troops in the Ghoul Wars...The acclaimed liberator of all Purgatory...Armageddon!"

The demons positively lose their freaking minds in a deafening cheer. My upper lip twists. *Screw Armageddon and his fake liberation of Purgatory. He handed us over to ghouls so we'd send more souls to Hell, pure and simple.* It's only when demon DNA mixes with a human that you get different powers. On their own, demons are mindless soul-munchers. My eyes flare red. I start to make a lewd hand gesture in Armageddon's direction, but Walker snags my wrist before I get too far. He shoots me a stern look, mouthing the words 'put a lid on it, Lewis.'

Nodding, I grip my hands behind my back. I'm enough of a warrior to know he's right: taunting Armageddon is a B-A-D idea. I focus on the ground, force myself to breathe slowly, and try to keep my cool. My inner demon has a mind of its own with more than my tail. When my eyes flare red, it's my demonic side getting rowdy. Sometimes, it's a struggle to keep it in check.

From his great stone throne, Armageddon watches the frenzied demon crowd, his thin red lips curling upwards. He scans every face, soaking in each expression and nuance, weaving them all into some complex and dark plan.

I shiver. He's being crafty again, and damn, that makes my skin crawl.

Raising his hand, Armageddon quiets the crowd. "Today's soul was a favorite of mine on earth. Unbelievable strength. No capacity for conscience. Pure untainted evil. When he wins this battle—which he will, make no mistake—then we'll finally have one of our own inside the gates of Heaven." The dark seats howl with glee while the angels collectively shiver. Grinning, Armageddon retakes his seat.

All faces turn to the Angel Verus. She slowly rises to her feet, her white wings spreading regally behind her. She shouts one word: "NEVER!" The force of her yell sets columns rattling and rubble tumbling to the ground. Her gaze turns to me, eyes flashing bright. Armageddon follows suit, his irises glowing red as he scans me from head to toe. A satisfied smirk winds the corner of his mouth. I've seen that look on other faces; it's the one that says '*that* little girl? Maybe she's won before, but against *this* opponent? Are you serious?'

Which pisses me off, big time.

Sharkie thumps his staff again; a human soul appears nearby. In life, this ghost was a man about six feet tall with broad shoulders and two-hundred fifty pounds of solid muscle beneath them. Now he appears as a spectral version of his mortal self: a ghostly hulk whose pale body looks ready to burst from his faded jeans and dirty white t-shirt.

Sharkie addresses the spirit. "Vincent Francis Morris, you've chosen trial by combat, is this true?"

"The Choker. My name's…The Choker." Squinting his piggish eyes, the ghost flicks a fat tongue over his full lips.

"I will ask again." Sharkie's irises flare bright red. "Have you chosen trial by combat?"

The ghost curls his hands into fists. "Yes, combat."

"Select your opponent." Sharkie grins, his knife-like teeth glimmer in the pale light. "First, we offer XP-22."

The Choker eyes our 'fighting ghoul.' With barely-there skin and the muscle tone of toilet paper, anyone could crush XP-22. In fact, the Choker would probably snap him in three seconds or less, but I don't think he'll choose to. Ghouls look mighty terrifying, even the weak ones. Most humans avoid them.

The Choker is no different. "I'll pass."

Sharkie moves his thin arm to the next figure in line. "Second, we offer Sheila, the Limus demon."

Sheila's fourteen red eyes whip about her upper body, finally stopping to glare at the ghostly human. She stretches wide the black hole that serves as her mouth, letting out a gurgling roar. When that girl puts her game on, she's terrifying.

"Hmm." The Choker's beady eyes give Sheila a long stare; the entire Arena seems to hold its breath.

I glance at Sheila and shake my head. Limus demons are almost as easy to kill as XP-22. The trick is, they're super-flammable. One match and you turn a six-foot monster into a puddle of harmless goo. But like XP-22, they look worse than they actually fight.

The Choker frowns. "Nope."

"And third, we offer the quasi-demon, Myla."

The Choker's eyes slowly scan me from head to toe, his creepy gaze lingering on the curves under my t-shirt and sweats. Rage shoots up my spine. What a scumbag. If he stopped thinking with his pants for two seconds, he'd notice my demon tail instead of my boobs and butt. Some quasis get stuck with pig- or bunny-bottoms, but I hit the jackpot: the long and thin variety with an arrowhead end. Even better, it's coated in dragon scales, so the thing's nearly impossible to block or cut.

But the Choker isn't being smart. He stares into my big watery brown eyes and long lashes; I shamelessly blink in fake-terror. For trial by combat to be valid, the soul must have a chance at winning. They get three options, two of which are relatively easy to defeat. Then, there's me, the one nobody should pick. Except they always do.

"I choose her." His thick mouth stretches into a vicious smile. "I'll fight Myla." In a low voice, he adds: "You'll find out why they call me the Choker."

I jam my hands in my pockets and fake-shiver. *And you'll find out why they called me to fight you, dickhead.*

Sharkie thumps his staff on the ground again, and the ghostly Choker turns into two-hundred fifty pounds of real human. "So be it."

~

End of Sample

Order ANGELBOUND today!

APPENDIX

If you're reading my freaking acknowledgements, chances are, I should thank you for something. So, for the record: you are awesome, dear reader.

That said, huge and heartfelt thanks must go out to my husband and son for their rock-solid support. Being an author means a lot of early mornings, late nights, long weekends, and never-ending patience. You two are the best guys in the universe, period.

After that, I must thank the extensive network of reviewers, friends and colleagues who helped me build my writing chops in general. Gracias.

Finally, deep affection goes out to my late, much loved, and dearly missed Aunt Sandy and Uncle Henry. You saw the writer in me, always. Thank you, first and last.

ABOUT CHRISTINA BAUER

Christina Bauer thinks that fantasy books are like bacon: they just make life better. All of which is why she writes romance novels that feature demons, dragons, wizards, witches, elves, elementals, and a bunch of random stuff that she brainstorms while riding the Boston T. Oh, and she includes lots of humor and kick-ass chicks, too. Christina lives in Newton, MA with her husband, son, and semi-insane golden retriever, Ruby.

Stalk Christina on Social Media

Blog:
http://monsterhousebooks.com/blog/category/christina

Facebook:
https://www.facebook.com/authorBauer/

Instagram:
https://www.instagram.com/christina_cb_bauer/

Twitter:
@CB_Bauer

VLOG:
https://tinyurl.com/Vlogbauer

Web site:
www.bauersbooks.com

www.ingramcontent.com/pod-product-compliance
Lightning Source LLC
Chambersburg PA
CBHW011240200726
48288CB00018B/3402